Married to the Lord
Samantha Holt

Edited by Dom's Proofreading

Proofed by Destini Reece and Em Petrova

Cover art by Book Wizz

Chapter One

IF AUGUSTA CROSSED her eyes just so, the dancers before her became a rather amusing blur of colors and movement. Their arms and their feet no longer seemed to move elegantly to the music, and glittering jewels and feathers appeared nothing more spectacular than something one would wear every day.

She uncrossed her eyes and glanced down at the jewels glittering on her wrist. Of course, she was not lacking in emeralds or flowers or expensive fabrics but what a waste they were. Henry was not even here; nor would he be. She was beginning to doubt her erstwhile fiancé would ever return for her, despite the promises of his family. Two years and no wedding date.

She blew out a breath. She was beginning to look foolish indeed. And the fact this was her friend Chloe's engagement ball just made things worse. Only a few months ago, Chloe had been as much a wallflower as her. She was happy for Chloe, of course, but she couldn't deny the news created this little gremlin of jealousy inside her that she wished she could rid herself of.

She was about to cross her eyes again when she caught Joanna Lockhart looking at her with a bemused expression. Augusta gave an apologetic shrug. "It makes watching the dancing a little less dull."

Joanna's lips quirked. She mimicked Augusta, crossing her eyes so that she looked mightily odd. She uncrossed them and grinned. "So it does. Though, Lady Thornbury just spotted me doing it and I do not think she is impressed."

Augusta giggled. Joanna was beautiful and accomplished and had been snapped up as soon as she had debuted—and was certainly the least likely to cross her eyes. But while she was in mourning, there was no dancing for her—leaving her at Augusta's side and likely horribly bored. Augusta was fairly used to not dancing but apparently Joanna had been popular amongst the *ton* indeed during her time.

To the left of Augusta, Chloe leaned in. "Are you laughing at Sir Percival's dancing or was something else amusing you?"

Augusta had not even noticed Sir Percival's dancing. She supposed that is what happened when one watched the dancing through crossed eyes. She turned her attention to the older man, whose arms and legs were as gangly as sticks and seemed to flail about like the ribbons on a maypole. Pressing her lips together as she watched him, she shook her head. "Poor Miss Humphries. It almost makes me glad I have not been asked to dance at all."

"Should you not be dancing, Chloe? It is your engagement ball after all," Joanna asked.

Chloe made a face. "You know I loathe dancing and Brook is with his mother at present. I'd rather be in the library." She peered around. "In fact, I might escape soon. Far better than dancing."

Augusta nodded vaguely but she was not certain she agreed. Though she did not much enjoy large gatherings, dancing could be fun and was a fine way to pass the time.

Unfortunately, it was rare she was invited to dance. Whether it was her engagement to Henry, her painful shyness, or her slightly plain looks, she was not certain. Perhaps it was just a culmination of them all. Either way, she lamented that this was what her life had become.

When Henry had proposed to her, she had envisaged a life much more exciting than this. If only she was a little bit braver. Then perhaps she could wear feathers and jewels and bright colors and attract the attention of someone else. Maybe that would teach Henry a lesson.

Joanna gave an audible sigh. Augusta grimaced to herself. If she thought her life was terrible, what did poor Joanna think? Her husband had died suddenly and without warning after a brief marriage only recently. No doubt she was missing him.

Augusta leaned over and tapped the back of her hand gently. "Would you like to talk about it?"

A gentle smile curved Joanna's lips. "I feel I have talked of Noah's death endlessly. Look, everyone is avoiding me as though I have some kind of plague."

"Well, we are here," pointed out Chloe.

Joanna gave their friend a look. "For now."

Chloe did her best to avoid balls at all costs, which was why it rather puzzled Augusta how she had ended up with a man like Brook who seemed to enjoy them so much. However, he was clearly besotted with her and she with him. Somehow, it worked.

Unlike her and Henry.

At this point, she might consider joining Chloe too. Every time she stepped into one of these events, she felt every set of eyes in Hampshire upon her. Oh, how everyone stared. Poor Miss Snow. Abandoned by her fiancé who was goodness knows where, doing goodness knows what. Last she heard he was in Spain. Her only letter from him had come all the way from some country that she had been forced to look up on the map. Only since the war finished did anyone go on The Grand Tour but it was rare an engaged man did so. And never for more than two years. She was beginning to look extremely silly indeed.

"I would be better off at home," Augusta muttered then clapped a hand over her mouth. "Forgive me, Chloe, I did not mean—"

Chloe snorted. "I would not blame you."

Joanna cocked her head and eyed Augusta. "Why on earth would you want to be hidden away?"

"Because I can feel everyone's pity."

Joanna nodded. "I feel it too."

Lord, here she was lamenting her own situation when Joanna's was far worse. She really needed to stop being so silly. "Joanna—"

"It is well enough, I promise. It is getting rather tiring, everyone treating me as though I might shatter at the mere mention of my husband."

"I very much doubt anyone pities you. You are both beautiful and accomplished women," Chloe said determinedly.

Augusta wanted to argue with that declaration. Joanna was indeed beautiful with her fair hair, elegant profile, and curvaceous figure. Augusta could not see the same in herself. Her hair was a rather uninspiring black. It seemed to absorb all the sunlight around her, eating up any kind of glow her skin might have.

She was tall—too tall for a woman—and had few curves at all. It took the tightest of stays to ensure she had any cleavage to fill out her gowns. She liked her eyes and her lips but when combined with the dullness of her figure and hair, she did not think she inspired much interest.

Something she suspected Chloe never cared much about. Her wildly curly hair was a vibrant red. It looked as though someone had suffered a battle to try to tame it most days. Nevertheless, Chloe was extremely pretty and far more interesting to look at than herself.

Augusta blew out a breath. All this pitying herself would get nowhere. How many months had passed by as she sat and wondered when Henry would return for her? She watched the many young women be guided across the dance floor, smiles plastered upon their faces. How many were genuine, she did not know, but she imagined many were. All of them shared the same dream—a dream that had been pushed upon them since they were young girls.

They all just knew they would make their debut and find the perfect man. Many of those girls might even fulfill that dream tonight.

She herself had fulfilled that dream. And yet it had not come to fruition. Much longer and she would be considered a spinster and upon the shelf. No amount of communication from his family or herself would encourage him to set a date. She balled her hands into fists.

Why, if she thought about it too much, she would get so...so...so bloody angry. How unfair it was that she should sit here and watch everyone enjoy themselves while she waited for

Henry to finish whatever it was he was doing. Why should he have all the fun?

Straightening her shoulders, she lifted her chin. Perhaps if she made herself look more available, she could find herself a dance partner. It really was time she began to enjoy herself again. If she was to have to wait another couple of years for blasted Henry, she could at least have a little fun.

Though Augusta tried to catch the eye of several men, none came her way. In fact, the three of them were given a wide berth. She let her shoulders sag. "This is why I prefer horses," she muttered to herself.

"And this is why I prefer books," drawled Chloe.

"I like people," sighed Joanna. "Just not at present."

A young woman caught Augusta's eye as she waved frantically from across the room. It took Augusta a moment to recognize her in her rather mature gown and fashionable hairstyle. Miss Worthington hastened over. "Oh, I am so glad you are here. I did not see you tucked away in this corner." Miss Worthington took Augusta's hands, forcing her to her feet.

"I thought it best to...well..." How did one explain that one had resigned oneself to being a wallflower?

"Did you hear the news? Mr. Rochdale proposed! We are to be wed before the end of summer."

Well, at least Augusta did not need to enlighten her friend as to why she was tucked away in the corner of the ballroom. She suspected she could have said almost anything and her friend would not have noticed. She remembered that feeling when Henry had proposed—that giddy, whirly, blurred sensation that meant everything else was dulled. Unfortunately, that feeling had long since passed.

Forcing a bright smile, Augusta squeezed her friend's hands. "Yes, I heard. I am so thrilled for you. He seems a good man."

Miss Worthington nodded vigorously. "He is such a good man," she enthused. "Mama and Papa approve of him greatly. After the wedding we shall be honeymooning in Europe and then travelling to his estate in Kent."

"Kent?" Augusta echoed.

"Yes, but of course we shall return to Town for the Season. And Mr. Rochdale has work in Hampshire." Miss Worthington squeezed Augusta's hands. "We shall still see each other, I promise."

Augusta's smile wobbled. How many times had she heard such a promise from her friends? Married life took up much of one's time. Her original circle of friends had changed so drastically and Augusta was left on the outskirts. She understood well enough that becoming a married woman changed one's life—and she was pleased for her friends, really she was—but she just wished she could join them finally.

"And I wager by next Season, you shall be wed too. What fun it will be! Two married women. Perhaps we shall even have babies."

Augusta could hardly visualize herself married let alone having babies. After Henry proposed, she had spent many a night picturing such things, but those imaginings had faded over the past years. Sometimes, she forgot what Henry looked like. She had to look at the little painting she had of him to remind her.

If she forgot what he looked like, he had no doubt forgotten her entirely. Did he even recall they were engaged?

But what was a girl to do? Once one was engaged, they were at the mercy of the man to whom they were engaged. She could not break it off—her parents would be heartbroken and no doubt gossip would circulate to why. It might be better for her to break things off than Henry—or else she would be entirely ruined—but it still left her with few options. She was an only daughter with no plans other than to marry.

"Do not be sad." Miss Worthington released Augusta's hands and cupped her face. "He shall come for you, I am certain of it."

Augusta forced her smile back in place. "I'm sure he will."

Miss Worthington snapped her head around at the sound of her name being called. "Oh, forgive me, everyone wants to congratulate me. I have never had so many people wish to speak to me in one night."

"Go, go," urged Augusta, shooing her friend away with her hands.

She paused to watch Miss Worthington disappear into the crowds, biting back what had to be the millionth sigh of the night. She really was over all this moping and waiting. It was high time she did something else with her time. But what?

She rejoined her friends. "It seems Miss Worthington has some good news. She is engaged to Mr. Rochdale."

Joanna nodded. "I had heard. They seem a good match."

"I had heard nothing. But I never seem to hear the gossip." Chloe peered at her nails and began to chew the corner of one.

"I cannot even remember who Mr. Rochdale is," she murmured around the end of her finger.

"He reminded me a little of Henry. They are the same age." Augusta frowned. "At least I think they are. It has been so long since I've seen the man, it is hard to say."

Joanna gave her a sympathetic smile. "I'm sure he shall set a date soon."

"I am losing hope of that ever happening." Augusta straightened. "But in the meantime, I'm determined to spend my time more wisely. All this sitting around the edge of the ballroom is becoming tiresome indeed."

Joanna chuckled. "That sounds rather like a vow."

"Perhaps it is." Augusta tilted her head.

To do lots of things was not in her nature. To talk with people, to dance, to explore all the various things in the world had always seemed so strange to her. She was much more comfortable spending time with just a few people and doing gentle things, such as walking or riding her horses. Solitary pursuits mostly. But those solitary pursuits had only reminded her of her unmarried status. Maybe it was time to change things.

"Perhaps," Joanna suggested, "you should show your fiancé what he is missing."

Chewing on her bottom lip, Augusta weighed the words. He was not missing much at the moment but could she possibly change? Become one of those vivacious creatures that every man wanted and every woman envied? It seemed almost impossible and, yet, she could not help but want to try.

"I suppose I could...be a bit more fashionable." August shrugged. "Mama would not object to new gowns at all."

Chloe narrowed her gaze at her. "You are thinking of powdering and primping yourself?"

"I know it sounds silly—"

"Not all," Chloe interrupted. "I think it is a fine idea. Far better than sitting around and waiting for that—" She paused and smiled. "For Henry to return."

"I could try to be more confident. Force myself to do more things."

"I can certainly help you and, of course, offer my aid as an escort." Joanna grinned. "We could be seen at all the right places to ensure word of how wonderful you are reaches Henry."

Augusta blinked. The plan began to take root in her mind. Somehow, she was going to pull herself away from being a wallflower and show Henry exactly who she was without him. With the help of these two women, it might very well work.

The smile that began to break across her face froze when her gaze landed on a dark-haired man pushing his way across the ballroom with a determined look on his face. Her heart gave a little jolt. What was he doing here? He rarely attended events like this.

His gaze latched onto hers. Her throat tightened. She stood swiftly, turning so that she nearly knocked into one of the chairs, then twisted the other way and bashed into Chloe's legs.

"Oh, forgive me. I must..." She could not finish the sentence. Not when he was looming upon her. She moved past Chloe with haste, aware of her calling her name. The room became a blur as she dashed past dancers and doors until she barreled through one and shut it behind her. Pressing her back against the cool wood, she took a deep breath and glanced around at the darkened confines of the empty room. How silly she was, but she could not face him.

It was too humiliating.

She could not fathom what Henry's brother might want with her; nor did she want to find out.

Chapter Two

PAUSING, MILES DEBATED his options. Follow Augusta and confront her as to why she might run from him or give up and turn around. He rotated on his heel. Why he should cause such wide-eyed fright in the petite girl, he did not know, but it was highly likely to do with his brother Henry.

Bloody Henry.

If only his damned brother would return and marry the poor girl. Lord knew, she had been waiting long enough.

He returned to the table where Walsingham and Roberts watched him with amused grins. He sank onto the chair and ignored the smug look in his friends' eyes.

"Not often we see a lady run away from you, Ashwick. It was quite a sight."

Miles glanced up at Walsingham and offered him a cold look.

Roberts chuckled. "I cannot deny it was not ever something I thought I would see."

Blowing out a breath, Miles finished off the glass of port in front of him. "I do not blame Augusta one jot for not wishing to speak with me. It seems the sins of my brother have been cast upon me. And Lord knows, she probably blames me for not ensuring that he has returned home to fulfill his duty to her."

Walsingham shrugged. "Henry has always been a free spirit. We were all surprised when he proposed to Miss Snow so quickly."

Miles clasped the empty glass, squeezing the delicate stem between several fingers. He had been surprised too. They had known Miss Snow and her family for decades and Henry had never shown any interest in her until her debut. One season later, and they were engaged. Miles could still remember his brother coming to him and telling him of his intention to wed her. His gut clenched even now.

He released the stem of the glass and forced his hands to relax. "Whether he offered for her hand too quickly or not, he made a commitment. I intend to ensure he sees it through. Somehow."

"Where is he at the moment anyway?" Roberts asked.

Miles shook his head. "By the time I receive his letters, he has moved on. Last I heard, he was in the Baltics."

"You could cut him off," Walsingham suggested. "He won't get very far without funds."

"I promised my father I would never do such a thing. Unfortunately, I think he was all too aware of Henry's nature before his death. Besides which, my mother would never let it happen. She would probably disown me first."

"She's a pretty girl, you ought to ensure he returns home with haste. She will not wait around forever." Roberts refilled all their glasses from the bottle.

If only that was true. He suspected the devoted Augusta would wait forever for Henry. If only she would break off their engagement it would solve all their problems, but she would never do such a thing. And he could not ask it of his brother or else he would scandalize her for life.

Even if it did free her of Henry. This foolish brother did not deserve the sweet Miss Snow one bit.

Miles watched the dancers in front of them, twirling gleefully with a joy he could not feel. He seldom attended events like this, but he had known Brook Waverley since he was a boy and could hardly turn down an invite to his engagement ball.

Walsingham leaned back in his chair. "You know, I thought you might offer for her once upon a time. You seemed rather sweet on her."

Miles was about to take a sip of his port. Thankfully he didn't or else he might have choked on it. "Offer for her?"

Walsingham lifted his shoulders. "Did you not have that history together? Spending time together as children etcetera?"

"It is hardly history. We did spend some time together as children, but I'm four years her senior and could hardly count myself as interested." The lie felt true enough seeing as he had told it to himself many a time over the years.

Roberts wagged a finger at him. "Now that's not true."

"I was never interested," Miles insisted.

"No, what I mean is that you do share history. You saved her life once, is that not right?" Roberts pressed.

Walsingham nodded. "Oh yes, I recall the story. She nearly drowned, did she not? I remember some piece about it in the papers years later—regaling you as some kind of hero."

Miles tried not to think of that day. He had been convinced that Augusta was dead when he hauled her from the lake at his father's estate. She had been thirteen and he almost an adult, and she had seemed so fragile in his arms. Thankfully he had managed to get her to cough up any water she swallowed and she recovered quite rapidly. But he did not consider that history as such. No, she and Henry had shared many more memories.

Perhaps, if he had not been so busy with taking up his position as viscount when their father had passed, he would have been able to step in and talk to his brother—ensure that the match never happened. Alas, he had been dealing with the grief of his mother, himself, and all that came with taking over his father's role—not to mention the mess he'd created by living a less than angelic lifestyle previous to his sudden elevation to lordship. He regretted deeply he had not been more involved in his brother's affairs.

Walsingham took a long draw of port. "Well, history or not, I would not be letting that woman out of my sight. Some scoundrel will swoop in and take her from your brother." Walsingham grinned. "If she were not your brother's, I could not claim that I might not be that scoundrel."

Miles narrowed his gaze at his friend. As much as they got along, Miles could not always agree with Walsingham's moral path. Miles might have lived a less than salubrious lifestyle in his early twenties, but he'd never seduced women at the rate that Walsingham did—if at all. However, his friend was right. He had returned home specifically to find Augusta after hearing some murmurings that she was tiring of waiting for his brother. Regardless of how he felt about anything, he could not see her harm her reputation because his brother was a fool.

He finished the second glass of port and stood. "As much as I hate to admit it, you are right, Walsingham. I shall go have a word with her friends over there. Perhaps they can apprise me as to her current state of mind. And I can find out if there are any other potential suitors waiting in the wings."

Roberts chuckled and lifted a glass in salute. "Good luck."

Miles cut a path across the dancefloor toward the two women. Waverley's fiancé looked extremely bored, while the other seemed uncomfortable. He knew of Mrs. Joanna Lockhart but did not know Miss Larkin all that well. Even as he approached, she did not seem to notice his presence. Mrs. Lockhart straightened her shoulders and offered a polite smile.

"My Lord, we do not see you in Hampshire much. It is a surprise to see you here tonight."

Miles dipped his head to both women. Miss Larkin peered up at him and brushed a red curl from her face. "You scared away our friend, Sir."

"Forgive me. It was unintended." He bowed. "May I offer my congratulations on your engagement, Miss Larkin. I am certain you shall be very happy."

A genuine smile lit across the woman's face as both women rose from their seats. "I think we shall."

"Viscount Ashwick is a friend to Miss Snow, I believe." Mrs. Lockhart eyed him. "Is that not true?"

"They did not seem much like friends," muttered Miss Larkin.

"It is true," Miles agreed. "I had hoped to speak with her."

"Do you have news of your brother? You know, she is quite fed up with waiting. You really ought to have better control of your sibling." A slight smile curved the Miss Larkin's lips as though she had enjoyed scolding him.

"Chloe," muttered Mrs. Lockhart. "I am certain Lord Ashwick is doing his best to ensure his brother fulfils his duties." Though Mrs. Lockhart's tones were dulcet, he suspected there was an edge to her words.

Not that he blamed either woman. It seemed Augusta had been explicit in her annoyance at being made to wait for Henry. It was a fine thing that he had come to Hampshire after all. He really did need to speak to Augusta and persuade her to wait for Henry. For all his brother's faults, Miles owed it to him to protect his interests.

"I have no news, I'm afraid. But I do wish to speak with Augusta on the matter. Let me assure you that I do not find it any more acceptable than she does."

"Well, I think you have scared her off for the night. You may have to find her another time." Miss Larkin waved a dismissive hand.

"I really would like to speak to her," he implored the two women, feeling as though he was addressing the gatekeepers.

"I'm quite sure you can call upon her." Mrs. Lockhart frowned.

He could. But then he would have an audience. If these mutterings of her discontent were true, he did not wish to reveal such things in front of her family. It was better that they spoke alone. Although they were in a room with a hundred people, there was enough noise to ensure that they could have a private conversation. Far easier than sitting in her drawing room with the door wide open to her parents.

"I am certain you understand that this is a delicate matter. There are things that Augusta might not wish to be shared. I was hoping I might snatch a little time alone with her. Do you perhaps know when she might be attending another party?"

Miss Larkin and Mrs. Lockhart shared a look. Miss Larkin gave a sigh. "Your best chance is to catch her riding close to home."

Miles nodded. Of course, it should have been obvious. Augusta had always adored horses. He would have to make a visit to her family's stables, perhaps even discuss the purchase of an animal with her father to give him a good reason to go there. It would give him a chance to keep an eye on her and have a private word or two.

After all, it was perfectly natural to wish to keep an eye on his brother's interests. This was nothing at all about wanting to see her. Even if he could not get that first glimpse of her after over two years out of his mind. He simply felt terrible for her. As Viscount Ashwick, he had a duty. A duty to this woman and a duty to his brother.

That was all this was about. Duty. And nothing else at all.

Chapter Three

ARMS PROPPED UPON THE fence, Augusta tilted her head and rested it against her forearm. From here, she watched the farrier lead the new horse around the paddock. Though the air was becoming tinged with the light chill of the approaching Autumn on some days, a shudder ran down her spine for which she could not blame the weather as it was quite temperate today. She squinted up at the sun, half covered by a delicate wisp of a cloud that did little to dampen its power. Certainly not the weather's fault.

No, the tremors attacked every time she recalled her behavior last night. She should never have run away from Miles. But how could she face him? It was all too embarrassing. He knew better than anyone that his brother had no interest in returning to her. At least in the ballrooms, the gossips did not know the truth. Certainly she overheard them pondering her fate. *Will he ever return?* they asked. *Why does he not set a date? Perhaps he has changed his mind?* But to all of those people, it was still questions.

To Miles, it was fact.

And if there was anyone she did not want to look a fool in front of, it was him.

She snorted to herself and lowered her head to press it against her arm. What a fine job she'd done of that!

If only she had never accepted Henry. She should have known it was too good to be true. Henry was charming, attractive, and though he was the second son, she was no lady. Her family had enough wealth and stature to hold their own, but she could never have expected to marry into nobility. She was beginning to suspect Henry had only offered for her out of grief or perhaps some sense of duty. His father had been sickening and passed away just prior to him asking her to marry him. If she looked back, his proposal was surely due to how muddled his mind had been. Augusta had been there, as a family friend, to offer a shoulder to cry on.

Apparently, that shoulder was no longer of interest to him.

She raised her head to see her father in the distance, riding his favorite horse around the fields that surrounded their home. Most of the land was either for farming or pasture and they owned a fair amount but nothing like the acres that Miles and his family owned.

"Are you not riding today, Gus Gus?"

Augusta twisted and smiled at her mother. "Not today, Mama. I think I am a little tired from the ball."

Her mother tilted her head. "You did not dance at all. How can you be tired?"

Augusta peered at her mother, who looked as fresh-faced as ever despite their arrival home in the early hours of the morning. None of them could have had more than five hours of sleep and were it not for the temptation to see the new horse, Augusta might have remained in bed past lunchtime.

Unfortunately, the idea of riding did not appeal today. Nothing seemed to appeal. She was feeling supremely sorry for herself, and she loathed herself for it. Had she not said yesterday to her friends that she would do better? That she would show Henry what he was missing?

She blew out a breath. The problem was, she did not quite know how to start. She had been quiet her entire life. Were it not for Henry offering for her hand, she could not have imagined how she might meet a husband. She had always rather hoped some bookish, equally quiet man might find her appealing and then they could live a quiet life together.

"Gus Gus?"

Augusta resisted the urge to roll her eyes at the nickname. Everyone had been calling her that since she was a girl and could not pronounce her own name. Though it did not usually bother her, she wished her mother would not call her it in public.

"I am well enough, Mama. I just do not feel like riding today."

Her mother shifted a little closer and pushed a strand of gray hair from her face. "Did someone..."

"Yes?"

She cleared her throat. "Someone say something?"

"Well, I imagine lots of people said lots of things. Conversation does tend to happen at a ball."

Her mother tutted. "You know that is not what I mean."

"I am afraid I am at a loss as to what you are saying."

"I saw that Lord Ashwick was in attendance last night. Did you speak with him?"

What she meant was, had there been any news of Henry? Oh how she hated to disappoint her family like this. They were almost more eager than her to have a date set.

Augusta shook her head. "I did not."

"It is unusual for him to bother with such events." Her mother leaned on the fence and Augusta joined her as they watched their father ride past elegantly. "Though he really ought to attend more. He is quite the catch and could do with a wife to help him with his duties."

Augusta scowled to herself. Miles had shown little interest in marrying, even though he would be a fool not to understand it was part of his duty. She was secretly glad in a way. Somehow, she could not bear to see him marry. It was most likely because if he married it would remind her of her still unmarried state.

Yes, that had to be the reason for the churning in her stomach when she considered him gaining a wife.

"Well," Mama said, "perhaps he shall attend the next event. You can speak to him then."

Augusta said nothing. If she could avoid him again, she would. Growing up, there had been few people she had admired more than Miles. He had always seemed so dashing and grown-up. How embarrassing it was for him to know Henry had no interest in her.

"Augusta?"

Augusta and her mother turned to find Joanna and Chloe approaching. Augusta allowed herself a little smile. Though her friends had expressed an interest in coming to view the new horse, she had not really expected them to come. Especially so soon.

Mama pressed a hand to Augusta's arm. "I shall leave you ladies to it."

Smiling her thanks, Augusta nodded to her mother. They had a close enough relationship that her mother understood how lonely and frustrated she was becoming, especially with all her friends marrying. Her fairly new friendship with Joanna and Chloe had made the Season in London all the more tolerable.

"I did not expect you to come so soon." Augusta joined the two ladies, dipping in greeting.

Joanna unlinked her arm from Chloe's. "It was my idea. I ran into Chloe at the tearoom and we decided we should make a day of it."

"And because Joanna is here, we need no escort." Chloe wagged her eyebrows.

"Can you show us the new horse?" Joanna asked.

"Of course." Augusta glanced at the paddock. "I think Mr. Jones has taken the horse back to the stables."

"I'm afraid I know next to nothing about horses," confessed Chloe. "My mother always despaired that I showed no interest in them as a child."

"Well you do not need to know anything about them to appreciate them." Augusta led them toward the stables. "Our horses are extremely friendly. I am sure you shall like them."

They finished a tour around the stables and strolled out toward the thin stream that cut across much of the estates in the area and would eventually lead to the River Wey. After a fall into a lake years ago, it was about the only body of water she minded being near.

The three of them sank onto the grass, and Chloe fished a pebble out of the stream and flung it back into the water. "The Lord Ashwick asked after you last night," she said.

"And Chloe scolded him heartily for scaring you away," Joanna added with a smile.

Augusta pressed her lips together. "I must have looked a fool."

"Not at all," Joanna assured her.

Augusta was not so sure. Scurrying away from her fiancé's brother had not been her cleverest of moves and was entirely unnecessary. She swallowed. "I suspect that he wishes to tell me that Henry has broken off the engagement."

Chloe gasped. "No!" "

"He's a damned scoundrel if he does." Joanna shook her head. "He shall ruin you."

Augusta bit down on her bottom lip, it was true. None would want to touch her after a broken engagement. She would most certainly be a spinster for the rest of her days. And yet, a vague sense of relief washed over her when she thought of the agony of waiting would be put to an end.

"There is little I can do about what Henry decides," she said more calmly than she felt. "But I can assure that I will come out of this with my head held high."

"You have nothing of which to be ashamed," Joanna said determinedly.

"I know. But..." Augusta twined her fingers together in her lap.

"But?" Chloe pressed.

"But there is this part of me, this part very deep down I suppose. That thinks I should come away from this...I do not know...somehow different." She untangled her fingers. "You know how we spoke of showing Henry what he was missing. Well, perhaps I can still show him. He might not just change his mind, but I would rather show the world that I am not shamed by his actions." She blew out a breath. "I'm so very tired of their pity."

Joanna nodded. "I understand, but what do you want from us?"

"I thought perhaps you might be able to help me be... Well, different."

Chloe narrowed her gaze. "You keep saying different, but what do you mean by that?"

"Prettier. More appealing. Not so blasted shy."

Chloe made a face. "I am not certain I'm the best person to talk to about this. I have certainly never been accused of being pretty."

"But you're not exactly shy," Joanna pointed out.

"I am hardly a beacon of confidence either."

Augusta gestured to Joanna. "You are always stylish, Joanna. You understand fashion far better than I do."

Joanna fingered her grey skirt. "Goodness, I miss fashion. At least maybe I should be able to indulge my interest in it with you." She leaned forward. "That is what you want, is it not?"

Heat tinged her cheeks. "I sound silly, do I not?"

Joanna shook her head vigorously. "Not at all. I would hope that if I were you in your position, I would do the same."

Chloe's lips tilted. "Well, I do rather like the thought of proving everyone wrong though I am not certain I can help."

Augusta opened her mouth to argue the matter then Chloe waved a hand.

"Nor do I wish to have any charms." Chloe grinned. "It looks like far too much effort."

"So, we shall dress you up and make you fashionable and show all exactly what Henry is missing. They can report back to him about how his fiancée is thriving without him." Joanna clapped her hands together. "You know, this is just the sort of project that I need."

Augusta released a long slow breath. Thank goodness the women didn't think her foolish. It was a strange favor to ask of someone, she was sure of that. In truth, she hardly knew where to start and at least with Chloe and Joanna's support she could be...different.

"Where...where do we start?" Augusta asked.

Joanna pursed her lips. "I do wish we had more time, but..." Joanna trailed her gaze up and down Augusta. "I may have some gowns that will fit you with a little tweaking."

"I did not even think about how we might do this with such short notice." Augusta nibbled on the end of a finger. "Perhaps this is impossible."

Chloe shook her head. "Nothing is impossible," she declared. "If I can manage to avoid dancing with a single man the entire Season, then you can do this."

"Excellent. So it is decided." Joanna took Augusta's hand. "We will guide you through this, regardless of what may happen. A few new gowns, a touch of makeup, and I am certain there shall be many men falling over themselves to be in your company."

Augusta squeezed Joanna's fingers, wishing she could feel the same. Her plan might not work and it might very well make her a figure of ridicule. No wallflower had ever managed to transform herself into the darling of society, but now that Chloe and Joanna were aiding her, it did not seem to matter so much. Perhaps if she could just prove something to herself, it would make her feel all the more better about this awful Henry situation.

"And now is your time to start..." Joanna's lips curved and she looked over Augusta's shoulder.

Augusta twisted and followed her gazc, her heart dropping down to her toes. No. Why did he have to be here?

Tall, wide-shouldered and walking with a confident gait, Viscount Ashwick was one of those men who commanded attention from everyone when he walked into a room. Even when strolling through fields, she could not keep her gaze from following him. There were few men who made her feel small, but Miles was larger than most men and his dark eyes always made her feel as though he was looking deep into her soul.

He strode over and greeted all of them. "I am glad you are here, Gus. I was hoping to speak with you."

"We can go back to the house if you wish." She gestured toward home, trying to ignore the flutter of nerves in her chest.

"I wish to speak with you alone. Without your parents watching over us."

Her lips parted, and she clamped her mouth shut and glanced around. "My father is not at home today but my mother is. You can say whatever it is that needs to be said in front of them. I do not mind." She lifted her chin. "I am not scared."

Mile scowled. "Why would you be scared?"

"I... I do not know."

"May we take a quick walk?"

She glanced at her friends, and Joanna made a little shooing motion and mouthed 'be brave' to her. Nodding, she allowed Miles to lead the way along the edge of the stream, further into the fields.

"I was surprised to see you by the water," he said.

"It is shallow."

"You still do not like water then."

"No," she admitted. "Not after..."

"Yes," he said tightly.

When she had been younger, she had been swimming in the lake on the Charlecote estate and her legs had cramped. Unable to swim, she had nearly drowned and had it not been for Miles's quick actions, she would have died. Now she could only regret her silly behavior that had put her in danger.

They strolled a little further along and Augusta fought for something to say. Be brave, Joanna had said, but how could she be around Miles? He had always seemed so worldly and wise and, at times, intimidating, even when she was younger.

"I was hoping to, uh, solve this situation."

"Situation?" Her mouth dried. This was it then. This was the moment she found out she was ruined and her family would be heartbroken.

"With Henry."

"I see."

"I understand if you are rather tired of waiting for his return."

"It has been some time," she said hesitantly.

"I hope that you will..." He sighed. "That is..." He paused and turned to face her. "You still wish to marry him?"

"Oh...of-of course." The response left her automatically. After all, what else was she to say?

"Good. Excellent. Well..." Miles rubbed a hand across his jaw. "Then, perhaps I can invite you and your family to dinner. Then we can...discuss things further."

"Yes. Naturally. Of course." She took a breath and forced herself to pause for a moment. "My parents would be delighted."

He smiled, the creases appearing around his eyes. "But not you?"

"That is not what..."

"I am teasing, Gus."

She rolled her eyes, trying to ignore the strange warmth that budded inside of her at the use of her childhood nickname. It had been many years since Miles had teased her and she should not like it but it rather reminded her of a time when life was much easier. She was not much looking forward to this dinner party, which she assumed was when he was to let her know Henry was breaking things off, but at least this might give her a chance to prove herself something more than a dull wallflower.

Chapter Four

MILES'S GAZE SLID TRAITOROUSLY toward his guest for at least the hundredth time that night. He regretted he was not hosting a bigger dinner. At least if there were more guests, his attention would not be snared by her so frequently. There was something wildly different about her. He could simply put it down to the jewel-toned gown she wore, seeming to fit just so. But it was more than that.

Seated between Mr. Simpson and Sir Cadbury, both of whom were charming men with good countenances, Augusta offered sweet smiles and the occasional bashful look. While he suspected his mother had planned it deliberately knowing how shy Augusta could be, whether it was the company of the two men, or something else, she did not seem nearly so shy as he expected.

He curled his fingers around his fork, letting the metal dig into his palms. Her laughter drifted across the table. He could not help but look again, taking in the slight blush on her cheeks and the way her eyes sparkled. She did not look like a woman waiting.

Damn it. Henry was going to ruin this girl. He wished his brother would just return and get this blasted marriage over and done with.

He shifted his attention down the table, toward Augusta's mother and father. They often dined with his mother but with how busy he was, he rarely attended dinner parties at the Hampshire estate. If her parents were as frustrated as Augusta was, they showed no sign of it. However, the families had been friends for many years and he suspected the Snows did not want to cause a rift between them.

Another peal of laughter snared his attention. He forced his gaze to the tablecloth, tracing the ornate pattern that was sewn into it with his gaze. He needed to get Augusta alone tonight. He had hoped it would be far easier to do at a dinner party than at a ball, and her parents would be distracted so there would be no chance of them listening in.

Of course, he should have just spoken to her at the stables but she had seemed reluctant to stay and converse with him. He did not blame her. It had been at least two years since they had seen each other and, apparently, those years had changed her more than he had realized. This vibrant woman seemed nothing like the quiet girl he had known before his father's death.

"So, Lady Ashwick, what news of Henry?" Lord Blyth asked. "I hear he is in the Baltics at present."

"Oh yes." His mother nodded eagerly.

Miles winced. He could not help but glance toward Augusta, whose gaze drifted to the cutlery upon the table. Of all the topics of conversation, why did Lord Blyth have to talk of his brother? Particularly with their current company. He suspected the elderly Lord was angling for some gossip and, unfortunately, his mother would fall straight for his trick. There was nothing she liked more than to speak of her beloved younger son.

"He has involved himself quite heavily in some of the charitable work there," she continued. "He tells me he is finding it quite rewarding."

Miles bit back a small snort. Henry was no cad but charitable work had never truly been of interest to him. He half-suspected a woman was the reason for his longer than necessary absence.

"We shall look forward to his return then he can regale us of his adventures." Lord Blyth glanced around the table. "You have quite the son there, Lady Ashwick. We are all on edge, waiting for him to grace us with his most excellent presence."

Miles ground his teeth together until his jaw hurt. He was well-used to Henry receiving praise—and if he was honest, sometimes Henry deserved it. After all, he had not involved himself in the deep belly of a dark underworld like Miles had in his early years. However, Augusta did not need to be hearing any praise of Henry right now.

When he looked up, he found Augusta's gaze upon him. She did not appear any more thrilled by the topic of conversation. Thankfully the conversation turned to more mundane topics as the desserts were served—sugar cookies accompanied by orange cream, baked apple pudding for those who preferred warmer desserts. Rice pudding, ices, and syllabub also made an appearance upon the table. Miles tasted little of it.

After the cigars and brandy, they rejoined the women in the parlor room. Miles waited until a few more sherries and such had been consumed before approaching Augusta.

"Might I have a quiet word?" He leaned down, catching the sweet scent of a floral perfume. He straightened swiftly when his traitorous gaze fell upon her cleavage. Clearing his throat, he gestured toward the open doors of the terrace that had been left open to clear air that was thick with cigar smoke and the lingering heat from the day.

Biting down on her bottom lip, Augusta nodded and rose from her seat. Her parents were too involved in conversation to notice their departure and, if his mother saw, she would say nothing.

The moon was full and bright, reflecting off the lake and rendering the tips of the trees around the estate a milky white, as though they were covered in snow. He stole a look at Augusta. He could not help but wonder if she still recalled the day that she had nearly drowned at his country estate. Did her stomach still churn with dread whenever she saw a large expanse of water? They had never spoken of the moment but he knew his still did.

She took an audible breath and turned to face the gardens once they reached the balustrade that dissected the terraced area from the rest of the gardens. Her hand shook and she clasped them together in front of her. Miles found himself fighting the desire to take her hands and squeeze them tight, to remind her that she had no need to be nervous around him, that he knew her better than anyone.

But did he? He had neglected to spend any time with his brother's fiancée since their engagement. Naturally, it was because he was far too busy.

Though the gnawing in his gut told him he was lying to himself. He loathed that Henry and Augusta were engaged. Deep down, he suspected he would also be frustrated even if they were happily married. As much as he would like to blame his brother's behavior for his discontent, he could not ignore the quick flutter of his heart and heat flowing through his veins now that they were alone.

He could not deny that he stayed away from her for a reason either.

Damn it.

"Whatever it is you have to say, just say it." Her voice trembled. "I do not mind."

He drew in a long breath of cool air, savoring the sweet honeysuckled tinge to it. If he said what was truly on his mind, he would likely frighten her away. Lusting after one's brother's fiancée was more scandalous than her sitting around waiting for Henry to finally set a date.

Miles swallowed hard. He turned his attention to the moon, the bright glow less painful to look at than Augusta. "I have heard talk," he began.

"Yes," she said softly, as though not surprised.

He pressed his lips together then found the courage to face her. Her eyes were wide in the moonlight, her skin pale. She was a tall woman but slender—on the verge of skinny. It made him want to wrap his arms around her and protect her from anything that might do damage. But the fact was, he could not protect her from the damage that might occur should she attract the wrong attention thanks to her dissatisfaction with his brother. All he wanted for her was to be safe and happy, regardless of what he felt.

"Gus." Her eyes widened at his use of her childhood nickname. But he did not feel bad about using it. How much easier it was when they were younger and he could speak to her freely, without fear of convention or society.

"Gus," he repeated. "I must caution you about doing anything foolish."

Her brows creased. "Foolish? I do not see how I am doing anything foolish."

He eyed her. "I do understand that you have been waiting a long time. But Henry will return for you."

She pressed her lips together. "Do you truly believe that, Miles?" She turned away and rested her elbows upon the stone balustrade. Lanterns lit around the gardens and the glow from the windows warmed her skin as the moon vanished behind a cloud, but it highlighted her frustrated expression.

Miles curled a hand at his side. There was nothing he wanted more than to provide her with comfort. To tell her he would fix all of this. Drag Henry back by his ear...or even his balls. Better yet, force her to break off the engagement and...well...

But she loved Henry. She'd *always* loved Henry. It had been clear to them all from when she was a young girl. If he could give her what she wanted, he would do it, no matter the cost to himself. However, he could not have her damaging her reputation in some misguided attempt at drawing Henry back to her.

"I do," he lied. "Why would he not?"

"I almost do not blame him for staying away." She peered at her gloved hands, turning them over to stare at her palms. "What can I offer him? He is out in the world, no doubt enjoying himself. If he returns to me—" She peered sideways at him. "I am not the sort of woman who can compete with the world."

"I never had you marked as a fool." He mimicked her posture, bringing his elbows to rest on the stone next to her. A few inches separated them and the scent of flowers teased him with each tiny breath of wind.

"Well that is comforting, thank you."

He chuckled at her vexed tone. "You think because you are quiet and shy, you have nothing to offer a man? Gus, that's preposterous." He slid a hand over hers before he considered the action, aligning his palm along hers. His fingers dwarfed hers, hiding the white satin gloves entirely. He slid his fingers between hers and she responded, curling her fingers so the fabric-covered tips entwined with his.

A silent thrill ripped through him, practically tearing his heart asunder. He should not be doing this. Should not be relishing this. Certainly should not be committing the feeling to memory.

She was his brother's fiancée. His brother's damn fiancée.

Still, he remained, her hand clasped in his. A contact too intimate for mere friends or almost relatives.

"I have my doubts. I cannot claim to relish being afflicted with such a temperament that I can never fully express who I am."

"Even to m—?" He caught himself. "Uh, even to Henry?"

She lifted a shoulder. "Henry shines brightly indeed. It is hard to appear anything but dull beside him."

"Gus," he said, his voice rough. "You are never dull."

Especially out here, with the breeze whispering through her hair, making her curls an impossible temptation to touch. She exhaled and he heard the frustration held within that one breath. She slowly unlooped her fingers from his and turned.

"I should go back inside. I told myself I would brood no longer."

"Gus, wait—" He moved swiftly, taking hold of her wrist, keeping her captive. Keeping her here. With him. He didn't even know what he wanted to say, what he could possibly say. Nothing proper to be certain. A riot of wholly improper thoughts raced through his mind followed by the burning temptation on his tongue to tell her how much he admired her, how beautiful, brave, and lovely she was.

"Miles?"

One syllable. That was all it took to unravel him. However, instead of spilling out his heart to her, he tugged her into him, finding it easy to draw in the slender woman until her free hand was pressed to his chest. She looked up at him, eyes wide and dark and intriguing. Soft-looking lips parted and a rush of agonizing need coursed through him, sending his very nerve-endings alight.

How many times had he thought of taking Augusta in his arms?

How many times had he tried to deny he'd suffered such thoughts?

There was no denying this moment, however.

"Miles?" she said again, the word whispering into the light breeze. The moon's cold rays cast over her skin, and his heart thudded heavily in his ears at the sight she offered. He released her wrist with every intention of turning away.

But she remained there, damn it. Lips still parted, eyes still wide. A picture of innocence and perfection that he wanted to get his sullied hands on.

"Christ," he muttered as he took her face in his hands, vaguely aware of the softness of her skin before he dipped his head and captured her lips with his. She uttered a gasp but he swallowed the sound swiftly, all the pain and frustration of never having been able to touch her before being channeled into his movements.

He kissed her fiercely. Hard. Desperately. She tasted of sweet wine and sugar. Her fingers curled into his shoulders and her hips swayed into his. Fire unfurled through him at these tiny responses. With a groan, he kissed her again and again, heedless as to their proximity to the drawing room, uncaring for whether they could be caught or not. One desire drove him—his need for Augusta.

Laughter shattered the air. Miles broke away even though she showed no sign of wishing to end the kiss, and the laughter was some distance away. He kept a hold of her face, letting her warm, ragged breaths wash over his lips. His chest rose and fell as he gulped down air. He rubbed his thumbs over her cheeks, looking into eyes that were clouded with confusion and—dare he believe it—desire.

"Gus," he murmured, resting his forehead briefly on hers before dropping his hand from her face. He should probably beg for forgiveness. Get on his knees and offer her penance. But how the hell could such a moment be wrong?

He shook his head, more at himself than anything. How did he let himself get in this situation in the first place? He should have known he would not be able to control himself once alone with her.

Her fingers came to her lips, touching them as though he had singed her with his kiss. She opened her mouth then shut it. He did not blame her. There was nothing that could be said. He dipped his head briefly and headed inside, fighting the desire to turn back and look at her...or worse, take her in his arms once more.

Chapter Five

AUGUSTA BLINKED, THE hazy light of dusk casting an eerie grey hush over the estate land—an unwelcome change from the warm lamplight from inside Charlecote House to her tired eyes. Her father handed her up into the open carriage and she greedily snatched the woolen blanket there, tucking it around her body and allowing her head to loll back against the soft leather interior. Smothering a yawn with the back of her hand, she lifted her head up long enough to look at the house then to Lady Ashwick.

Her parents offered their *thank yous* for her so there was no need for anything more than a polite smile, but she should not have been hungrily hunting the windows for any sign of Miles.

She let her head drop back again and hitched the blankets up around her neck to keep out the morning chill. Was it her imagination or did her lips still feel hot? She resisted the urge to touch them for the hundredth time that night. She had done it so many times that her mother had asked her if there was something wrong. No, she had said, shaking her head vigorously and adopting a careful smile while lacing her fingers firmly together, ensuring that they remained prisoner and could not betray her again.

It was a lie, of course. There was most certainly something wrong. That sense of it fluttered there, like a trapped bird in her breast, thudding hard in her ears and against her rib cage. Wrong, wrong, wrong. She should never have responded to Miles's kiss. Should not have even stayed out there unaccompanied with him. It would be slightly less than scandalous that she was alone with her fiancé's brother, but there would be no saving her from ruin if anyone had spotted them.

Oh Lord. She pressed both hands to her stomach but the tension would not be suppressed. They really could have been caught too. While they were surrounded by friends and family who cared for them, there had been enough people in attendance who would probably enjoy the scandal that followed from such a moment. They would pretend that they were shocked and terribly sorry for her parents that she had been caught acting so wantonly but they would be quick to ensure everyone—especially Henry—knew of the act.

Her mother slid into the carriage beside her, offering a warm body to lean against. Wrapping an arm about her, her Mama added another blanket and brushed a soft kiss against her head. Augusta's heart panged and she guiltily snuggled into the offered embrace. Her parents would be utterly appalled if they knew what she had done. Why, oh why had she not turned away? Why had she kissed him back? Miles was a gentleman and would never have forced a kiss upon her. All it would have taken was one word, one small action. All these years of waiting and she had nearly ruined everything with her fiancé's brother!

The carriage rocked and creaked on its suspension as her father climbed into the barouche. Through half-lowered lids, she watched him wave vigorously while the vehicle jolted forward and crunched its way down the road out of the estate. Augusta eyed the sky lazily, watching it give way to morning. She would retreat to bed for a few hours once she was home, though she was not certain she would be able to sleep. Not while her lips still tingled and certain little spots on her body were hot with remembrance.

Trees came into view and the crunching beneath the wheels gave way to the smooth sound of metal gliding over dry mud. Birds chittered in the trees above, excited to start a new day. She wished she could feel the same. She *should* feel excited—after all Miles had said nothing of the engagement being called off. She was not ruined and left on the wayside.

She must have dozed as they reached home far quicker than she had anticipated. Rubbing her eyes then stretching, she reluctantly gave up the blankets in exchange for her father's hand. She yawned and yawned again as she clumsily climbed down from the vehicle. Her mother gave her a quick squeeze. "Go and rest a while but do not forget we have a few people coming over for an 'at home' today."

Augusta peered at her mother. "How is it you look as though you have rested a good twelve hours, Mama?"

"Because I have much more practice at dinner parties than you do, my dear, and I know when to conserve my energy." She smiled. "But that does not mean I will not take to my bed immediately, and no doubt your Papa shall be snoring to the high heavens in his study chair before long."

Too tired to summon a response, Augusta nodded and took the few steps up to the house, grateful for the warmth that wrapped about her as she stepped into the long entranceway. Built in the Elizabethan era, the walls were lined with dark wood paneling and each door was fashioned out of the same dark-stained oak. It was no dramatic Georgian entranceway like that of Charlecote House, but she appreciated the comfort the smaller room brought. When she stepped into the main room, light spilled through the one huge window, casting colored patterns on the stairway as it simmered through the stained glass that edged the top of the glass. She grumbled her discontent at the invasion of daytime. "Can you not stay away a little longer?" she muttered as she made her way upstairs and ducked through the low doorway into her room. At least then she would not have to face what she had done.

Only bothering to remove her gloves and fling aside a few pins from her hair, she tumbled into bed and wrapped a sheet around her body, cocooning herself as though that would somehow prevent her from thinking of Miles. But, of course, nothing could cease her rambling, slightly crazed thoughts of that kiss.

Sweet Mary, even thinking of that word...kiss...it was too much. It made heat flow to her cheeks and her limbs turn to liquid. She had never received anything more than a chaste peck from Henry as he bid her farewell before his travels. It had been a wonderful moment, she had thought, and had kept that memory close for some time. Now she felt silly for thinking of it as anything other than a little dull. Miles's lips upon hers had banished all thoughts of Henry's.

She tossed onto her front and buried her face into the welcome feathery softness of the pillow. It did little to comfort her. Every slide of cotton against her skin, every touch of fabric, and she was reliving how Miles held her face, recalling the taste of his lips, remembering how hard his body had felt against hers. How hard and yet...how wonderful. How protected and cherished she had felt. How out of control and wild it had been and yet whenever she felt she could lose her footing, she would find his arms there, holding her just so and ensuring nothing happened to her, preventing her from being carried away.

Though so much of her had wanted to be carried away.

This was so, so terribly wrong.

As she closed her eyes, she could not help revel in it and take herself through every moment all over again. She let herself be back on that balcony, feeling the thrill of their fingers entwined together, seeing the intensity in his eyes and not knowing quite why it was there but wanting to know what was behind it anyway. She let his fingers slide over her face again, allowed him to hold her so that she could not get away. Augusta watched him lower his mouth to hers and did nothing to escape it.

She knew, without doubt, that if he tried to kiss her again, she might very well allow it.

Sleeping fitfully, she arose with a dry mouth and gritty eyes. She looked at the clock on her mantelpiece, blinking several times to clear the fatigue from her eyes before she could make out the time. She only had an hour to prepare for visitors, and Joanna would be there so she wanted to be punctual. A far too talkative maid aided her in dressing and doing her hair but Augusta welcomed the brutal tug of a brush through her hair, making her scalp tingle and rousing her to her senses a little more. She grimaced when she spotted the dark shadows under her eyes, made all the more stark by her dark hair. Still, at least she was not seeing anyone who would care if she looked a little worse for wear.

At least she was not seeing Miles.

Goodness gracious, why did his name have to be summoned into her mind at every interval? He had not even bid her farewell. Clearly he knew it had been a huge mistake too. She was not even certain why he had kissed her. He was far too interesting and experienced to want to kiss her, surely?

Precisely. So that was another excellent reason to put it out of her mind. Why he had kissed her, she did not know, but there was no doubting it was a mistake on both of their ends. Better to forget it and think on how exciting it would be for Henry to come home. With any luck, the renewed pressure from his brother would ensure his return by winter and they could set a date. How very, very exciting.

She forced a wide smile once the maid left her bedroom and gave a little curtsey to herself in the mirror. "Mrs. Henry Stanton," she murmured experimentally. "Mrs. Henry Stanton." She made a face at her reflection. It did not seem nearly so wonderful as it once had. "Mrs. M—"

No! That was not acceptable.

Spinning away from the mirror, she left her room and headed downstairs to the parlor room. Two of her mother's friends had arrived early but there was no sign of Joanna yet. She joined the ladies and listened in silence as they discussed the gossip that was surrounding a particular young woman who was rumored to be having a dalliance with a stable hand. Augusta had little interest in such gossip so she contented herself with drinking as much tea as possible to quench her tired and dry mouth until Joanna arrived.

Though she should not be envious of her friend, it was hard not to. No signs of the late night marred Joanna, and her perfect skin practically glowed as though she had slept beautifully for a whole night. Augusta rose to greet her and they seated themselves away from the growing crowd of older ladies.

"How is it you never look tired?" Augusta asked, picking at a slice of fruit cake and discarding the sultanas on the plate.

"I am exhausted," Joanna groaned. "Utterly, bonelessly tired." She grimaced. "In fact, I genuinely cannot tell you the last time I felt this tired. Once I returned home, I fell into such a deep sleep that I forgot what day it was."

Augusta was not certain whether her friend was trying to make her feel better or not so she turned her attention back to the remnants of her cake.

"Augusta," Joanna said.

She lifted her head. "Yes?"

"Is there a reason you have barely a word to say to me?"

Augusta glanced into Joanna's knowing eyes. How she could appear knowing was beyond Augusta. There was certainly no chance Joanna really had any inkling of what occurred, but her friend always proved extremely intuitive. After all, she had been the one to recognize that Chloe was in love with Brook while Augusta had not known such a thing until Chloe had admitted it herself.

Augusta blew out a breath. If she did not say something, she might very well explode, and she had little desire to lie to a friend. But would Joanna judge her poorly for her behavior? She had to hope not.

"Augusta?" Joanna prompted.

"I kissed Lord Ashwick," she whispered, the words hurried.

"Pardon?"

Glancing around, Augusta patted her mouth with a napkin to mask the words. "I. Kissed. Miles."

"Good Lord."

Several heads spun in their direction and Joanna patted Augusta vigorously on the back. "Not to worry," she said gaily, "just a little crumb. Scared us both." Joanna leaned in toward her, keeping her voice low. "Of all the people to do such a thing, I never expected it to be you."

"I never expected it to be me either," Augusta muttered.

"When? How? Why?"

Augusta lifted a shoulder. "Out on the balcony. I do not really know how. Nor do I know why."

"Good Lord," Joanna repeated, albeit quietly this time. She pursed her lips. "Was it a good kiss?"

Augusta very nearly did choke on her cake this time. "Joanna!"

"Well, it seems a sensible question to ask. If it was not good, I would hardly think you would be sitting here, squirming as though you have a scandalous secret."

"It *is* a scandalous secret and it would be even if the kiss was terrible."

"So it was not terrible?" Joanna waggled her eyebrows.

"Oh Lord...I should never have said a word."

"Do not say that." Joanna grasped Augusta's hand. "Tell me, how was it? And how do you feel now?"

"It was...spectacular," she admitted on a sigh. "And I feel terrible."

"Spectacular," Joanna echoed. "How wonderful."

"It is not wonderful. I'm engaged to his brother for goodness sakes," she hissed.

"Well, if Henry did not want you kissing other men, he should be here, claiming you for himself." Joanna pressed a finger to her lips. "Though, Lord Ashwick does have quite the reputation for being a naughty chap."

"I do not think he is so naughty these days..."

"Still, it has to be more fun than waiting around for Henry."

Augusta eyed her friend. "I really thought you would have something useful to say to me."

Joanna laughed. "It seems that kiss has made you quite spirited. I rather like it."

Augusta groaned and Joanna laughed again. "It is all very well for you to laugh. You did not do something utterly scandalous."

"No one saw you and I am certain Lord Ashwick would never tarnish your reputation by speaking on it. Anyone can see he holds you in high regard."

Augusta frowned. "Do you think so?"

"Oh certainly." Joanna plucked up a slice of cake and took a sizable bite. "What a shame you fell for the younger brother because the older one is quite attractive in a brooding way. A shame he is such a naughty chap too."

"I do not think he is naughty..." Augusta protested half-heartedly again.

Though she could not argue with Joanna. She was beginning to wonder why she had ever fallen for Henry when a man like Miles even existed. However, it was no lie that Miles had been engaged in quite reckless behavior in his past life. She never knew all the details but had heard rumblings of disapproval from some of the older members of society.

Tearing another sultana from her slice of cake, she blew out a breath. Her best hope was to put the kiss from her mind and continue with her scheme to live her life a little less...dully.

Well, she supposed she had already achieved that. Just not in the way she had expected.

Chapter Six

MILES COULD COUNT ON one hand how many garden parties he'd attended. They'd certainly never interested him when he was younger when gaming tables, women, and drinking had been more his style, and he forever felt out of place at them now. However, he'd spent over a week avoiding anything that Augusta might be attending and was beginning to feel foolish.

Or more like an ass.

Either way, he had to face her at some point.

When he spotted her, he knew he had not been wrong to come. She was wearing a light lemon-yellow dress and had flowers in her hair. She perfectly matched what was turning into a fine day and seeing her was like a damned punch to the gut. Somehow, he'd pushed that kiss out of his mind, burying it in work and the occasional whiskey. Now it came back to him, sucker punching him with all the force of a heavyweight opponent. He could taste her lips, feel her lithe body, recall the little noises she made. His fingers itched to press into her hair and pull it down around her shoulders.

He'd have a fight on his hands, though, even if she were not bloody engaged to his brother. Apparently, he was not the only one to appreciate her dress and delicate hairstyle. Three men surrounded her as she stood by the fountain. Miles noticed her two friends keeping their distance though watching with interest. Damn them both. They should be protecting her, not watching these blasted men fall all over themselves to speak with her.

He ground his teeth together and weighed his options. One of the men was Edward Jenkins, heir to a shipping fortune and new money. It didn't matter much to Miles where his damned money came from, but it did matter that the man had a reputation for ruining young ladies like it was a sport. Even if Augusta was not engaged to his brother, Miles still would not want her getting involved with someone like Jenkins.

There was no missing the scowls of the other men as he entered the group. Augusta's gaze flew to his face, her eyes widening. "Miles," she said breathlessly.

"It is nice to see you, Augusta," he said, dipping his head and inserting himself bodily between Augusta and Jenkins.

"You...you too."

He almost regretted coming closer. She wore a little makeup that emphasized her dark eyes and full lips. Clearly, he had not learned his lesson as he found himself wanting to drag her away to another balcony and kiss her all over again. If they were not standing in Sir Clifton's garden, surrounded by likely one hundred people, he was fairly certain he might try to take her in his arms again. What sort of an ass of a man had such thoughts about his brother's fiancée? Sometimes, he suspected he had not changed so much from his younger years as he liked to think.

"Anyway," Jenkins said boldly, "you should most certainly come. Invite your friends. Mrs. Lockhart can act as chaperone, can she not?"

"Chaperone?" Miles asked.

"Oh, just a little soiree," Jenkins said, waving a hand. "We have just opened up Carlton Manor for the summer. You must know it, Ashwick. It has quite the reputation."

Miles clenched his jaw at the title-less use of his name. He rarely cared for formalities but he and Jenkins were not well-acquainted enough for speaking as though they were friends. And he did know of the house, which had been let out to the Jenkins' family for quite the price. It was over the border in Surrey and too far for Augusta to travel with just her friends as far as he was concerned.

"I do know of it, Mr. Jenkins," he said with emphasis. "I used to spend time there in the summers when the Ferriers owned it. A fine house indeed, if in need of modernization."

Augusta issued a tiny gasp and Miles regretted the petty jab.

"I am certain Miss Snow here would appreciate the gardens and the house." Jenkins kept his gaze fixed firmly on Augusta and Miles could not help glower down at him.

The man was average height and attractive in a polished manner with fair hair and even features. The smile he offered Augusta left Miles in no doubt as to why innocent women fell for him. Miles could not claim to understand the techniques these men used to charm women but it clearly worked. A slight blush had worked its way into Augusta's cheeks.

"They do sound wonderful," she admitted. "I have always had a hankering to visit Carlton Manor."

"Well, then it is decided." Jenkins shot Miles a smug look. "I shall send an official invite soon."

Miles cleared his throat and Augusta reluctantly looked his way. "I wonder if I might have a word," he asked.

She opened her mouth and he knew she intended to make an excuse.

"It is about Henry. Your *fiancé*," he added with a look toward Jenkins.

The man did not seem abashed but Augusta's cheeks reddened and she nodded, following him away from the crowd of men who appeared sorely disappointed at losing Augusta. Damn them all. They had no right to even look at her like they did. No right to talk to her, to invite her to soirees.

Christ, not that he was any better. He was probably looking at her exactly the same way.

"Do you have news of Henry?" she asked once they reached a rose bush, budding with pale pink flowers. She touched one of the petals with gloved hands, avoiding his gaze, and his whole body ached with the need to rip off those white gloves and feel her bare fingers against him rather than a damned flower.

"I needed to speak with you."

"So this is not about Henry?"

"Gus, look at me."

Her gaze eased reluctantly over to him.

"I..." He groaned inwardly. "Let us walk a little," he offered, indicating down a path that led between more rose bushes. He was a coward, but the problem was, he did not feel one jot sorry for the kiss. Sorry that he had betrayed his brother to be sure, and sorry that he could have damaged her reputation. Not sorry for the actual kiss. If things were different...

But they were not. Despite Augusta's sudden interest in the opposite sex and willingness to kiss him, deep down, she loved Henry. And why should she not? He might be a little wayward but he was handsome, charming, and a good man. Miles owed him a hell of a lot. Without Henry, Miles might very well have been dead in a gutter a few years ago. Really, it was right that Augusta and Henry were together. They deserved each other very much. If only he could persuade Henry to actually come home and claim her.

All his problems would be solved then and he wouldn't have to think on the kiss ever again.

They strolled in silence for a while. A gentle breeze brushed the ribbons of her bonnet, sending them curling around her face. She swept them aside with a little annoyed grunt and Miles tucked his hands behind his back to resist the temptation of sorting them out for her. When they came to where the path branched off and too far away from the party for their time together to be proper, Miles stopped. Augusta looked at him expectantly with dark eyes that made him wonder if she could see inside his soul—see quite how dirty and black it was. Though, she should have figured that out by now. There were few good men who would kiss their brother's fiancée.

"I must apologize for that night..."

She blinked at him. "What night?"

The words hurt, jabbing straight into his heart like a pointed spear. Surely she remembered?

He cleared his throat. "The night where I...uh...kissed you."

"Oh."

Her lips formed a lovely 'o' shape that made him want to take her face in his hands again and kiss her until he had her knees trembling and her body capitulated to him. Damn it. He shouldn't have walked this far or taken this long to gather his courage. It would be far too easy to slip off somewhere without anyone noticing. He could dirty her skirts and muss her hair to his heart's content.

God, he really was a cad.

"Anyway, I wanted you to know that I regret that action. Deeply. You...you are my brother's fiancée." His throat tightened over those last words. "Even if you were not, to kiss you like that, in public...it was utterly unacceptable."

"I see."

"You do not forgive me?" He shook his head and smiled. "Of course you do not. And I have no right to expect it." He eyed her. "Gus, how is it you can make a man feel even more heartily ashamed of himself with but two words?"

"I do not mean to make you feel ashamed, I swear it." She plucked a leaf from a nearby tree and twined it between her fingers, keeping her gaze lowered.

"I think perhaps you take a little pleasure in it."

She lifted her head. "You tease me!" She flung aside the leaf. "You know I would never take pleasure in such a thing."

"Perhaps." He gave a half-smile. "But at least then I get a response from you."

"I..." Her chest rose as she took a breath and he could not help but watch the enticing movement. "I accept your apology."

"Good."

"And I think it best we forget the whole matter. Call it a moment of madness, if you will."

"Madness? Yes, I suppose it was something like that."

Augusta certainly seemed to bring him to the edge of insanity but he doubted she understood quite how or why.

She smiled but it did not reach her eyes. "I do not think it serves either of us to dwell on it."

"So you shall put it from your mind then?"

"Absolutely."

"What a fine thing it is to know one can be put from Augusta Snow's mind with such ease," he drawled, unable to help himself.

"If you are trying to imply I have any ability of wounding your ego, Miles, I would call you a liar." She lifted her chin and eyed him head-on. "You are a titled gentleman with above average looks and a fine way about him. I am certain there are many kisses in your past and in your future, and you shall forget me quite readily."

"I am glad to know I have above average looks."

"Oh." She lifted her hands and threw them down. "You are determined to be obtuse today."

"Forgive me. I am done being obtuse." He lifted a hand. "I swear it."

She pursed her lips. "Very well."

"We had better head back to the party before you are missed." He glanced sideways at her while they followed the rose-scented path back to the main gardens. "Mr. Jenkins is likely missing you a great deal."

"I doubt he is that bothered by me. There was plenty of pretty young women in attendance."

"Still, I think you should be wary. Jenkins has quite the reputation."

"I know many men with reputations." She arched a brow.

"Yes, yes, I am a fine one to talk but please, Gus, be careful of him. I should hate to see something happen to you."

"What? Like be kissed by him perhaps?" she asked archly.

Miles almost smiled at the barb. It was rare the prickly side of Augusta made an appearance but he had rattled her quite hard, it seems.

"Just be careful," he urged.

"You are not my keeper, Miles."

No, he wasn't, and she should be grateful, because if he was, he'd keep her damn well locked away from every man and have her for himself. He sighed inwardly. This talk had done nothing apart from make her mildly annoyed with him and demonstrate one thing—he was as obsessed with Augusta as ever.

Chapter Seven

"I AM NOT CERTAIN I can do this." Augusta stilled at the bottom of the steps that led up to Carlton Manor.

Dressed in sandy bricks, tall columns, and high pediments that jutted out with all the dominance of the bow of a ship bearing down upon them, she could well understand why the house had such a reputation.

"Maybe Miles was right," she murmured to herself upon hearing the chatter and laughter emanating from one of the open windows. It was still early—only three o'clock in the afternoon—but it sounded as though some guests had been drinking for a while already.

"Come on, Augusta," Joanna urged, taking her arm. "There is no chance I am travelling all that way back home without at least a peek inside Carlton Manor."

"You'll be fine," said Chloe, who was accompanied by her fiancé Brook. "After all, we are here with you."

"I promised your parents I would look after you all," agreed Brook. "Jenkins is known for some rather...boisterous events but I vow I shall not let anything untoward happen."

"Why else do you think Brook came?" Chloe said, her brow arched. "He does not trust us alone."

"Was it not you who complained of being invited, Chlo?" Brook's lips curved. "Something to do with preferring to stay home and read?"

Chloe tapped her fiancé's arm with a gloved palm. "We are here to support Augusta."

"And support her we will." Brook shot a dashing smile her way and Augusta could well understand why Chloe had fallen for him. Dark-haired, handsome, and with a charming—if flirtatious—manner about him, he seemed to bring out the best in Chloe.

Well, they seemed to bring the best out in each other. Augusta imagined that was rather the perfect concoction for a marriage.

It did warm her cheeks, however, to know that Brook understood the reasonings behind her sudden interest in parties and gatherings. It was a little embarrassing that one had to practically change oneself to get a fiancé's attention. Not that it was working. There was still no word from Henry and only Miles seemed to be paying any heed. That was certainly not what she wanted.

Was it?

No, absolutely not. Straightening her shoulders, she walked up the steps with Joanna. They entered into a grand marbled hallway, large enough to fit a small house in. Nude statues in various poses of pleasure were tucked into corners and Augusta looked away. Her mother would think such a thing was in terrible taste and Augusta could not help agree. She appreciated fine artistry as much as anyone but there were some things that should not be used to greet one's guests.

A butler took their coats and ushered them into the drawing room. Augusta's mouth dried. When Mr. Jenkins had said a little soiree, she had foolishly believed him. Instead there were at least forty people spread between two drawing rooms. The doors at the end of the first room were pushed wide open, allowing her to see almost all of the guests. As they walked in, heads turned in their direction and she wished she could shrink until she was a mere few inches high then scurry away like a mouse.

"Goodness, this is quite the gathering," Joanna murmured.

Augusta blew out a breath. Had she not vowed to cease being the shy, quiet mouse who would rather scurry away and be unnoticed? If she left now, she'd prove Miles right—that she did not belong amongst these people. Even though there was the tiniest part of her that had been glad he cared where she went, she could not let him dictate her every move. Especially if she was ever going to get Henry home.

Mr. Jenkins approached, revealing a flash of white, even teeth. He was attractive in a carefully polished manner. She suspected he took a great deal of time over his appearance, which she supposed was better than taking none at all but it led her to believe he could be quite vain.

Unlike Miles.

Lord, where did that come from? She had told him she would forget anything ever happened and yet here she was, comparing other men to him. What folly.

Mr. Jenkins greeted them all then fixed his attention on Augusta. His blue gaze made her feel a little breathless but not quite in the way he likely hoped. Although she was certainly getting better at engaging with men, it still left her feeling all hot and flustered, and her hands shook a little, making it hard to take the offered glass of sherry when a servant came around.

"So, do you like the house?" he asked.

"It is certainly beautiful."

"It was built for royalty originally but it seems old George tired of it too quickly."

Augusta nodded. "Yes, I had heard."

"I should like to take you on a tour of it later," Mr. Jenkins said, leaning in a little too close.

"I am sure we would be delighted," Joanna replied for her, keeping Augusta's arm tightly linked with hers.

Mr. Jenkins smiled again but the smile did not reach his eyes. "Well, do enjoy yourselves. We have plenty to eat and drink and, as you can see, some of the finest company in the country."

Augusta glanced around at the men and women gathered. Indeed, there were some well-known faces in the room. Most were younger and highly fashionable. Many of them could be found in the gossip columns too. As much as Augusta wanted to show Henry she would not wait around for him, she was not certain she wished to end up as a line of text.

She and Joanna strolled around the room while Chloe accompanied Brook, who had met some old friends. Joanna laid a hand on Augusta's arm. "I knew of Mr. Jenkins reputation but this crowd is quite the insalubrious one."

"I fear you are right."

"Well, at least we can say we have seen the house and attended the party. Surely Henry will hear of this and you can consider it another success in your plan to show him what he is missing."

Augusta grimaced. "It sounds so frivolous and silly when you say it like that."

"Not silly," said Joanna, sinking onto a spare chaise longue that sat beneath one of the open windows. A fresh breeze washed over Augusta's bare neck and shoulders as she sank next to her friend onto the plush velvet. It made her itch to be outside, riding horses, and/or walking. Anything other than being here.

She glanced around at the guests. All were dressed fashionably and appeared to be having a riot of a time. This was not her. Oh Lord, this was really not her. What had she been thinking?

"Augusta, as a woman, one must do whatever she can to secure her future. You should have no shame in wishing to prove to Henry that he cannot just leave you here all alone. Any man should be lucky to have you." Joanna's lips tilted. "You have already proven yourself attractive to other men."

"Do not say it."

"Miles could not resist you, could he, after all." Joanna's smile turned mischievous. "Imagine what Henry would think if he knew."

"If he knew, he would never return and I would be ruined forever," Augusta said glumly.

"All I am saying is that you are an excellent catch and I am glad Miles recognized it, even if he is not the man for you."

"I'm not sure what Miles recognized." Augusta tweaked the seams of her gloves until they were perfectly straight.

Joanna gave her a little nudge. "That he cannot resist you."

"I doubt it was that. Miles is far too....well...far too something for me. And we both vowed to put that moment from our minds so I would be grateful if you do not bring it up again."

Joanna sighed dramatically. "A widow has to find entertainment somewhere. Is it wrong for me to enjoy that my friend is finally getting the attention she deserves?"

"I am beginning to feel utterly foolish about the whole matter. Especially now M—"

"Especially now Miles is paying you attention."

"Well, I certainly did not expect anything so...so messy to happen."

"Let us forget the matter, as you said, and concentrate on our plans to ensure you have some fun while waiting for the useless Henry."

"He is not useless, he is just..." Augusta let her shoulders droop. "He is just busy, that is all," she said softly.

Of course, the words sounded ridiculous. For so long she had been defending Henry, pretending there was good reason for him being gone for so long. After all, he was a good man. Everyone who met Henry said as much. He was about the nicest man she had ever known and she had known him all his life and it made sense that they should be together and...well there were so many reasons, it was hard to name them all.

Not to mention she had waited this long.

"I see those gentlemen appear interested in you, Augusta. I think it is the new hairstyle. It is quite becoming against your features."

Augusta could not deny that the softer look that her maid had created for her today brought out her lips and accentuated her long neck. She had almost felt like her hair no longer swallowed her whole once she was dressed and made up for the day. It was a lot of work, however, and she was not at all certain she could keep up these habits forever.

She glanced over at the men in question who were gathered near the empty fireplace. She recalled two of them from the garden party but could not for the life of her remember their names. Unfortunately, seeing Miles had just about erased any useful information all together from that day.

Swallowing, she nodded. "I suppose we should appear interested."

"Yes, let's. The taller one is quite handsome." Joanna looked at them boldly, her smile inviting. Augusta attempted to do the same.

Joanna glanced at her. "Perhaps I should do the inviting. You just look out of the window and appear disinterested."

"I thought I was meant to look interested."

"Well, some men like disinterest. It presents a challenge."

With a shrug, Augusta turned her head and peered out of the window to look at the rear gardens. They were likely glorious but she was too aware of the men approaching from the periphery of her vision. Joanna was right—the men liked her appearance of disinterest. Lord, would she ever understand the opposite sex? At least with Henry it had been simple. She adored him and he claimed to like her very much. She was not so certain now. It had been at a strange time in Henry's life that he had proposed and looking back, she rather suspected he had done it to assuage some of his grief over his father's death. Still, they knew each other well and there had been no need for flirting or pretending interest or disinterest.

Joanna gave her a nudge with an elbow and Augusta scowled before realizing the men were upon them. Augusta hastened to rise from her seat and greet the men. Out of the corner of her eye, she saw Brook watching them carefully—taking his role as chaperone seriously indeed.

"It is a pleasure to see you again, Miss Snow," said the taller man.

Augusta murmured something vague in response while frantically hunting her mind for the names of the gentlemen. The information had vanished, though, and she did not think anything could summon it back. The men did not seem to mind and engaged her and Joanna in conversation of hunts and riding—the men doing the majority of the conversing. After a while, Augusta's mouth hurt from smiling and her feet were beginning to throb in her attractive but too tight shoes. She looked about the room and realized the party was dissolving into something more, with cards being played for what looked to be large sums of money and the volume of the laughter and chatter increasing with the consumption of vast amounts of alcohol. She caught Chloe's eye as she stood rigidly next to Brook, neither of them appearing happy about where this party may lead.

"Joanna," Augusta said quietly, "I think Mr. Waverly may be ready to leave."

Joanna shared a look with Augusta and nodded. "I think you might be right. Forgive us, gentlemen, but our escort has another engagement."

A few protests went up but Joanna successfully disengaged them from the men. Before they reached Brook, Mr. Jenkins stepped in front of them both. "Not leaving already?" His words were slurred and his skin shone with sweat. His jacket had also vanished along with his cravat. Any pretense of being a gentleman had appeared to have vanished.

"Yes, we must be going." Joanna smiled politely but made to move past him, taking Augusta with her. "Thank you so much for—"

Mr. Jenkins put his hands to Augusta's waist, twirling her away from Joanna into some sort of waltz-like dance. She gasped and tried to push his hands from her waist but he kept a firm grip on her, twirling her and twirling her until she grew dizzied. "I must show you the house," he said when he finally stopped.

"Mr. Jenkins..."

"A private tour. What do you say?"

"Mr. Jenkins, I really—"

"I suggest you release Miss. Snow," came a deep voice. She looked to see Brook glowering down at Mr. Jenkins.

"We are just having a little dance, Waverly," Mr. Jenkins said dismissively.

"Unhand her or I shall be forced to make you," Brook said between clenched teeth.

The golden-haired man glanced Brook up and down and she felt his hold ease enough for her to slip away.

"You shall just have to come back for a tour another day," Mr. Jenkins said brightly. "Without your ogre here keeping guard hopefully."

Brook curled a fist and Augusta whirled away, not bothering to respond to their host. Chloe tugged on her fiancé's arm and they left the building swiftly before a fight could break out.

"I should not have agreed to bring you here," Brook muttered. "I could see where this damned party was heading an hour ago. I should have forced you all to leave."

"You know very well you could not force us to do anything we do not wish to do," Joanna pointed out. "Besides, we did what we needed to do. Augusta attended another party where she garnered quite a lot of attention. There were plenty of people there who know Henry. Word of her success will spread, I am certain."

Augusta shuddered. She was not certain she wanted news of her attendance to such an event to be talked of.

"Do not be disheartened, Augusta," Joanna said. "We shall make your Henry return, I promise."

Augusta nodded slowly but she could not help wonder if she really wanted him back.

Chapter Eight

HE KNEW VERY WELL WHAT he was doing when he came here but Miles still felt a fool when he spotted Augusta riding back toward her house. When he'd spoken to her father with regards to the Henry matter and promised to try harder to bring Henry home, he'd half-hoped she would be at home.

He'd also hoped she would not be.

Either way, it left him in a tangled mess.

Blowing out a breath, he redirected his horse and headed toward the stables so he could speak with her. She deserved to know that he had discussed this Henry situation with her father. He also wanted to find out what had happened at Jenkins' party. He'd already heard from Brook Waverly that her afternoon at Jenkins' had been disastrous. Waverly also mentioned that Augusta was quite popular with several gentlemen there. He tightened his grip on the reins and his horse gave an uncertain couple of steps to the side. He forced himself to relax. At least Waverly had been there to ensure nothing untoward had happened. But, damn it, Henry needed to return home—fast—before something else happened.

He dismounted when he reached the stables. Augusta must have already taken her horse into the stables. The long brick building was modest compared to his own stables but still housed several horses, such was the family's passion for them. He paused at the open doorway, hearing voices coming from the stall at the right. It only took him a moment to realize Augusta was not conversing with a groom but that bloody Jenkins. The man had some gall to be sure.

Miles eased around the doorway and waited for his eyes to adjust to the shadows. Three stalls down, he spotted Augusta, who faced him and Jenkins. Augusta tried to move past the man but he stepped in front of her.

"I thought you would be happy to see me," Miles heard him say. "I was saddened you could not stay at my party." He laughed. "It turned into quite the event."

From what Miles had heard, half of the guests ended up retreating to rooms for less than proper reasons. He was only grateful Brook had the sense to see what was about to happen and ensured they left safely.

"Mr. Jenkins, if you do not mind—"

Augusta didn't see Miles but made another attempt to move past Jenkins. He grabbed her arms and crushed her against him. Miles waited no longer. In a few short paces, he had Jenkins by the back of his neck, hauling him away from Augusta. The man spluttered and protested, but Miles didn't hear a word. He'd seen the grip he'd had on Augusta, the desire in his eyes, the determination to have her no matter what. Every inch of him was hot with anger. He balled a fist and struck him hard across the jaw. The sound of the contact echoed off the bricks. Somewhere in the back of his mind, he heard Augusta let out a cry.

Sprawled on the ground, Jenkins lay there for a few moments, dazed. Slowly, he eased himself up onto his elbows.

"Damn you, Ashwick, that hurt. Can't a man have a little fun with a beautiful woman?"

"Not that sort of fun." Miles ground his teeth together. Were it not for Augusta in the periphery of his vision, he'd likely lay the man out with another punch. He flexed a fist then thrust a finger in Jenkins' direction. "Come here again and I will call you out. And I warn you, I am known for being an excellent shot."

Jenkins looked Miles up and down then glanced at Augusta. Cradling his jaw, he climbed to his feet. He opened his mouth to say something then closed it, shaking his head and walking out of the stables. Miles waited until he was certain Jenkins was gone before turning to Augusta. She rubbed her arms where Jenkins had held her.

"Did he hurt you?" Miles glanced down at his own knuckles that were red and throbbing. Not painfully enough for him to feel satisfied though. The bastard deserved more than a punch for his behavior. Augusta might not have understood how close she was to being ravished, but Miles recognized Jenkins' determination too well—he'd spent time with men like that in his past and he regretted ever breaking bread with them.

"Just a little pinch."

He pushed up her sleeve to see the red marks that would likely turn into fingerprints. "Bastard," he muttered, regretting the word when Augusta jolted. "Forgive me."

"There is nothing to forgive. Thank you," she whispered.

"He has no standards, that man."

"I realized that. Unfortunately not quickly enough. You were right to say I should stay away from him," she admitted.

"If it helps, I take no pleasure in being right."

She looked up at him with a little smile and tugged down her sleeve. "I am not certain I believe you."

"Very well." He motioned with his fingers, indicating a small amount. "I take a tiny bit of pleasure in it but it is most minuscule I promise."

"What are you doing here, anyway?"

"A pleasure to see you too," he said, his lips tilted.

She gave a reluctant smile. "Forgive me. I just did not expect to see you."

"I was here to speak with your father about Henry."

"Oh."

There it was again. That lovely 'o' shape that made him want to press her against the bricks and capture her mouth with his.

"I have promised him that I will do my best to ensure Henry returns." His throat tightened. "To you," he added, his voice gruff.

"Oh," she repeated.

"I would have thought you would be glad."

"No, I am. Of course. It's just..." She sighed. "Do you, perchance, have time for a quick stroll? I doubt my parents will notice my slightly longer absence."

He should say no, of course. It was too dangerous for him to be alone with her, as he had so proved.

"Yes," he said, his own voice betraying him. Damn it.

They headed toward a coppice, set away from the house, in silence. The shadowy entrance beckoned them inside, offering privacy and a little shade from what was proving to be a warm day. Miles said nothing, too aware of his own heartbeat and her proximity for his liking. As soon as they entered the meandering path that sliced through the modest gathering of trees, his awareness of her heightened tenfold. Perhaps because they were alone. Hidden. Out of view. If he so wanted, he could kiss her again and no one would ever know.

He blew out a heated breath through his nostrils. And, damn, did he want to.

Sneaking a sideways glance at her, he forced his expression to remain neutral. She had already suffered enough with that bastard Jenkins today. The last thing she needed was her fiancé's brother muddying the waters yet again. Apparently he was not nearly sorry enough about kissing her because all he could think of was pushing her up against a tree and tasting that sweet, sweet mouth once more.

Augusta slowed her pace and finally came to a stop when they came to an almost circular barren path in amongst the trees. She sank onto a fallen tree with a sigh and peered at the canopy above. Afternoon sunlight dripped through the leaves, speckling her in golden dapples. Miles's mouth dried. Fire raced through his veins. Now he had enjoyed a taste of her, all he wanted was more. The mere thought of never touching her again, never feeling her body against him...not to mention watching her as his brother's wife made his insides feel as though they were being scavenged by wolves. Each moment with her was like another swipe of claws. Slowly, he was unravelling.

He straightened his shoulders. Which was why he needed to bring Henry home and put an end to this. Once they were married, he could make himself scarce. Spend some time in the house on the coast perhaps. Wherever they were, he would ensure he was not.

Augusta picked a dandelion and blew at the seeds. A few fluttered to the ground and she began to pluck them off in little bunches, dropping them by her feet.

"Augusta," Miles prompted. As much as he could spend all day watching her doing the most mundane of things, he did have business to attend and the less time they were alone together, the better.

She stopped and dropped the plant, offering him a meek smile. "Forgive me." She swiped her hands down her skirt and stood, closing the gap between them once more. "You said you were here to speak to my father about Henry?"

He nodded. "Yes, I—"

"I was hoping I might get the chance to speak with you about him."

"Well, you can speak with him yourself."

Augusta blinked. "What do you mean?"

"I finally have word that he is returning home."

She drew in a long breath. "He is returning home?"

"Indeed," he said tightly, searching for the excitement in her gaze. It was there, was it not?

"Home?" she repeated.

"Yes?"

"To here? From where he was?"

"Henry is returning to Hampshire," Miles confirmed.

Augusta put fingers to her mouth. "Why?"

"I am assuming to fulfill his obligation to you." His jaw hurt as he forced the words out.

"Well, I suppose..." She glanced at the floor. "I suppose that is good news."

"Yes, yes it is."

For her and Henry at least. Not for him, though.

Chapter Nine

"IS IT TRUE?" CHLOE demanded.

"Is what true?" Augusta asked.

"That you have a..." She glanced around the busy tearoom. "Attachment to a certain viscount," she hissed.

Augusta clapped hands to her cheeks. "Pardon?" Surely she must have heard wrong.

"Chloe!" Joanna scolded.

Chloe shrugged. "Far better for her to hear it from us than someone else."

"Whatever do you mean?" Augusta demanded, peering between her two friends who appeared decidedly uncomfortable. A rare thing indeed for Joanna.

Chloe waited until an old couple passed by their table and leaned in across the embroidered tablecloth. "Brook said there was talk of you getting, um, close to...Lord Ashwick." She mouthed the last part.

A chill ran through Augusta, spreading down to her toes and making her release a little shudder. Her vision felt fuzzy for several moments while her heart picked up its pace. Surely no one had seen them kiss? And the only person she had told about it was Joanna. She trusted her friend implicitly.

"Where did Brook hear this?" Augusta asked, her voice husky.

"From a friend of his—Lord Benedict?"

Joanna grimaced. "Lord Benedict could have heard it from anywhere. He is quite the sociable character."

Augusta resisted the urge to drop her forehead to the table and instead pinched the bridge of her nose. She could not fathom how Lord Benedict might have heard of such a rumor as he had not been in attendance at the party that night. Which meant it had to come from yet another source. And the more people who had heard such a thing, the worse it would be. It only took the faintest whisper of scandal to ruin a lady and an assignation with the brother of a fiancé was certain to ruin her, whether it be true or not.

Unfortunately, it was true. At least as far as the kiss was concerned. They might have vowed to put it behind them and pursue a completely innocent relationship as brother and sister-in-law but it would not matter if word continued to spread.

"Do you know what was said?" Augusta asked, her chin wobbling slightly. She clamped her teeth together to prevent it from happening again.

"There were no details but Lord Benedict came to Brook out of kindness, knowing of our friendship." Chloe reached across the table and rested a hand over Augusta's. "Lord Benedict hardly knows you but you can be assured if he believes you above reproach, then so will everyone else." Chloe laughed. "How could anyone believe such a rumor?"

The chill vanished and was replaced with a swift heat, spreading its way rapidly through her body and up into her face.

Chloe narrowed her gaze. "Augusta?"

Joanna gave a subtle lift of her shoulders when August glanced at her for support.

Augusta removed her hand from under Chloe's and reached for the delicate china cup in front of her. She drained the last drops of tea before placing it unsteadily back onto its saucer. She took a breath, checked that no one was within earshot, and leaned in. "I kissed Miles," she admitted. "Or he kissed me. Or we kissed each other."

Several heartbeats of silence passed over the table, punctuated by the clatter of teacups and the chatter of gossiping ladies. It still seemed deafening in its absence of sound.

"Goodness," Chloe breathed.

"I know." Augusta closed her eyes briefly and willed away any tears. What sort of a person was she, kissing her fiancé's brother? Or letting herself be kissed? Or...whatever it was.

What was even worse was when she had been alone with him yesterday, she had wanted him to kiss her again. She had been about to tell him that she was ready to end things with Henry. That, regardless of what he felt, she could not do it, especially not after falling so easily into Miles' arms. But then he had announced Henry's return and she could only thank God she had not said a thing and appeared an utter fool.

"Was it...nice?" Chloe asked.

Augusta blinked. "I...well, yes."

"Better than Henry?"

"Henry never really kissed me before he left," she admitted.

"Henry is a fool," Chloe muttered.

"He is n—" Augusta stopped herself. She was done dashing to his defense.

Chloe topped up their cups from the teapot in the center of the table. "Does anyone else know of this kiss?"

Augusta looked to Joanna.

"She knew before me?" Chloe shook her head and pouted. "How unfair."

"Chloe—"

"I am jesting." Chloe gave Augusta a little nudge with her elbow. "Though I hope you planned to tell me eventually."

Augusta dropped two sugars into her tea and added milk, stirring it for far too long and watching the tawny liquid swirl about the cup. "I am deeply ashamed."

Chloe arched a red eyebrow. "*Henry* should be deeply ashamed for neglecting you for so long."

"I know you think I am silly for waiting for so long. But none of this matters anymore. Not Miles, not these rumors, not the...kiss. Henry is returning home soon."

"I do not think you are silly." Chloe shook her head vigorously. "You are just a more patient and dutiful woman than I am. Those are not bad traits."

"Precisely," Joanna agreed.

"But you do not think I should marry him?"

"I did not say that. Did I say that, Joanna?" Chloe asked.

"I know that is what you are thinking. I know it is what a lot of people are thinking." She turned her attention back to her untouched cup of tea.

"We will always support your decisions, Augusta," Joanna assured her. "You know that. If marrying Henry upon his return makes you happy, then you should do that."

"That is if he still wants to marry me," Augusta muttered.

"He would not break off the engagement and ruin you, I am sure. His brother would not allow it for one," Joanna stated firmly.

Augusta suspected Joanna was right. Miles would never let anything bad happen to her. Why could she not have turned Henry down and...well...nothing, she supposed. Miles was determined Henry should return and marry her. That had to mean any feelings for her had long passed—if there were any feelings at all.

"With any luck, once you marry Henry, these rumors shall fade," Joanna said. "Though I would be careful not to be seen alone with Miles again."

Chloe grinned. "And no more kissing."

Augusta tried to smile at the teasing but it felt forced. Especially when all she could think of was kissing Miles again.

"Let us talk on more pleasant things," Augusta suggested. "How are your wedding plans coming along?"

Chloe made a face. "Mama is trying to make it the biggest event in all of Christendom, I think." She smiled. "Though, Brook is rather excellent at managing her I've found. I trust he will keep it the small affair we have hoped for."

"Soon, you shall be planning yours, Augusta," Joanna said. "Perhaps Chloe will be able to help."

"I hardly know what I am doing with my own. I'm leaving it entirely in the hands of others. I fear I would be useless!"

Augusta gave a weak smile but struggled to pay attention to the rest of the conversation. It could very well not be long until she was planning her own wedding. But did she even want to? It would solve many problems—both families would be happy about the connection and she would be looked after with no concerns for her lack of inheritance. Even Miles seemed pleased his brother was returning.

Had this news come even a mere six months ago, she might have been delirious but things had changed. *She* had changed. The time passed and her small increase in confidence—and the kiss from Miles—made her feel like she was almost an entirely different person.

They finished their tea and headed out toward the carriage, which was waiting by the fountain on the outskirts of town.

"Are you worried?" Joanna asked, as they walked along the cobbled road toward the waiting vehicle.

"About the wedding?"

"No, the rumors."

"Oh." Augusta pressed her lips together. "I suppose so." Though, honestly, as awful as they were and how much they could impact her, she had buried that concern under her thoughts of Henry returning.

"Perhaps you should speak with Miles," Joanna suggested. "He may have confided in someone and that is where the rumor came from."

It was hard to imagine strong, stoic Miles confiding in anyone, but *she* had told Joanna so why would she presume he might not do the same?

"I suppose I ought to."

Joanna grinned. "Here's your chance."

Augusta stilled. She had not noticed Miles on horseback, riding from the direction of town.

"I am not sure I should," Augusta whispered. "If we are seen together..."

"Lord Ashwick," Joanna greeted brightly.

"Mrs. Lockhart." He tugged on the brim of his hat. "Miss Larkin." His gaze landed upon Augusta and a tremor ran down her spine, making her feel as though she had turned to liquid. "Miss Snow."

Was it her imagination or did his voice deepen at the mention of her name?

"We were just about to take a little stroll and stretch our legs before returning home," Joanna announced.

Chloe scowled. "We were?"

Joanna ignored Chloe and Augusta's imploring look. "Perhaps you might accompany us?"

He glanced at Augusta, who could not decide whether to look away or meet his intense dark gaze. She did the latter, though hardly of her own will. His gaze sucked her in, leaving her powerless in his presence.

"I think perhaps I should—" Miles indicated down one of the country roads leading away from town.

"Nonsense." Joanna indicated for him to dismount. "I insist you join us. After all, who knows what ruffians we might meet along the way? Your company will surely offer protection."

Augusta winced. Their small town was known to be extremely safe and it was a rare occurrence that any ruffians stepped foot in it. Miles would know that. But, she supposed

Joanna was doing her a favor. She did need to speak with Miles about these rumors, no matter how embarrassing it might be to discuss that night. If he could find the source of them, he could put a stop to them before it did any damage to either of them.

Miles gave a tilted smile. “If you insist.” He dismounted and led his mount by the reins. “I would never forgive myself if you were hurt by ruffians because of your lack of company,” he said dryly.

They strolled along the country road that would eventually lead to Chloe’s house. Joanna controlled much of the conversation, giving Augusta little time to speak with Miles. It gave her too much time to sneak sideways looks at him, though. His broad shoulders and strong profile kept sending little shivers down to her stomach that blossomed into something sweet and hot at the same time. He glanced her way and she cast her gaze to the ground.

Once they were farther away from town, Joanna and Chloe dropped back a little, leaving Miles walking at her side. She gulped down a breath and willed her heavily beating heart to slow. “I-I have heard a rumor,” she announced.

“Oh yes,” he said. “Was it a good one?”

“Not really.”

“Well, that’s a mighty shame. Whoever cast it about must be a useless gossip.”

“No, that’s not what I—” She peered at his amused expression and rolled her eyes. “Miles, the rumor is about us.”

“Us?” A dark brow lifted.

“Yes.”

“What about?”

Oh Lord, he was going to make her say it. Her face heated. "About...us spending time together."

"Time together?" he repeated.

She threw her hands up in the air. "I have said it before and I'll say it again, why do you enjoy being so obtuse?"

"Perhaps I simply cannot help myself and do not do it out of pleasure. Perhaps your company ties me in knots and all I can do is speak obtusely, Gus."

She groaned aloud. "I do not know why you cannot resist teasing me even on the most serious of matters."

"Very well." He adopted a stern expression. "I am all seriousness now. Explain to me what is happening."

She pursed her lips and eyed him, seeing that flicker of a curve to his lips. "Apparently there has been talk that we might be forming an...attachment."

He chuckled. "Is that it?"

"Says a man who will never know the fear of being ruined," she muttered.

"Forgive me, Gus, that was wrong of me." He paused, and when Augusta glanced back, she realized they were unaccompanied on the road. She had seen Joanna do the same with Chloe and arrange time alone with Brook but this was different. She did not need or want to be alone with Miles.

Not one jot.

Especially when she found herself looking at his mouth and remembering how it felt upon hers.

"Where exactly did you hear this rumor?"

"Chloe told me of it. Apparently, Mr. Samuel Benedict came to her fiancé with word of it."

Miles nodded. "I see."

"Miles, you did not tell anyone of...well..."

"The kiss?"

She bit down on her bottom lip and nodded.

"I told no one."

She blew out a breath. There was no chance Joanna would have said a word to anyone so the rumor had to be speculation and completely baseless. But why would someone wish to spread rumors about her?

"I will speak with Benedict. See if I can discover the source of this gossip and put a stop to it."

"Thank you, Miles. I would appreciate that."

"Anything for you, Gus, you know that."

His jaunty smile made her want to cry for some reason.

Chapter Ten

"I SUSPECT I KNOW WHY I am here."

Miles watched Brook Waverly set down his hat as he joined Miles in the drawing room. The more masculine of the rooms, this had been Miles's father's preferred room, decorated in dark-stained walnut, red, and gold.

Miles waited until Waverly was seated then joined him while a footman poured them a dash of whisky each.

"I thought you might."

"Miss Snow," Waverly said simply.

Miles nodded and took a sip of whisky, savoring how it warmed his insides. He tried not to touch alcohol much these days but at the moment, he needed the comforting warmth. He'd tried to make light of these rumors and he was fairly certain no one really knew he and Augusta had kissed, but he could see she was fearful of the damage they might do. He'd promised her he'd do what he could to protect her reputation and he meant it.

He knew without doubt he would do anything for her.

And there was his problem. It meant he could never tell her of his feelings for her. Never hope that there was some slim chance she might really want him instead of Henry. She and his brother were meant to be together, of that he was certain. They matched well and despite Henry's failings as a fiancé, he was certain he would make a good husband. Augusta would no doubt be sublimely happy once married to him.

What more could Miles ask for?

He blew out a breath and forced aside any thoughts of having her for himself.

"I'll be frank, Waverly, you said there were rumors about us?"

"Benedict came to me. Thought it was best that Miss Snow hear it from one of her friends. I know little save from the fact there was talk at one of Benedict's dinner parties of your closeness and that perhaps Henry had waited too long and she was growing close to you."

Miles grimaced. It was speculation on the behalf of whoever had put the rumor about as they had hardly been seen together at all but Augusta's recent increased popularity with the opposite sex may have sparked notice.

"Did Benedict say where it came from?"

"He could not." Brook took a sip of whiskey. "His wife overheard it but could not name the source."

"So there are plenty of people who have already heard of the rumor." Miles pressed fingers to his forehead. This was not good news. For women, sometimes it only took a whiff of a scandal to ruin them. He'd been foolish in even going near Augusta. What if someone had seen how he looked at her and made the assumption? What if he was not nearly as good at hiding his feelings as he thought?

"Unfortunately so," Waverly concurred.

"My brother is returning soon," Miles said. "His ship should be docking in Southampton any day now."

Waverly nodded. "I had heard." He leaned back against the red velvet chair. "I would think that a wedding would put to bed any rumors. If Henry sets a date quickly, surely everyone will forget such gossip?"

"I can only hope." Even if the idea of them hastening down the aisle made his heart feel as though it was splintering in two. "I would hope they do not start their married life off on a sour note."

"If I were you, I'd find the source of the talk." Brook finished his drink and set the glass down on a gilded serving tray, set in the center of the coffee table. "If you can get them to admit they were lying, it would go a long way to protecting Miss Snow."

"You must have read my mind. Do you perchance know who was in attendance at Benedict's party?"

"The Livelys, I believe. And a few of the new crowd. You should ask Benedict but he is in Bath for the next few days."

Miles sighed. He doubted the Livelys, who were decent and fairly quiet folk, would have anything to say. The *noveau* rich, however... "Was Jenkins there?"

"Jenkins? Probably."

Miles shook his head. He knew precisely where the rumors had come from. No doubt it was revenge for Miles punching him the other day. He should have known someone like Jenkins would stoop so low as to try to damage a good lady's reputation. The chances were, if he did not put a stop to it, Jenkins might even do worse.

"It sounds as though you need to pay someone a visit," Waverly commented, rising to his feet.

Miles stood too. "My thanks, Waverly."

"Try not to kill the man," Waverly said with a grin. "Just a few bruises should do it."

"I won't kill him and I have my doubts he'd even consider a duel."

"I'll be your reluctant second if needs be."

Miles shook his head. "I have a suspicion your wife-to-be would not be impressed."

"You're probably right, but the offer stands."

Miles saw Waverly out then ordered his horse saddled. He could ride out to Carlton Manor swiftly enough, though it would be an easier journey in the carriage. But he suspected Jenkins was more likely to be staying close by, particularly if the man was intent on doing damage to Augusta.

There were few places for men like Jenkins to enjoy themselves in Hampshire—for the most part it was a quiet, country life and their town had a reputation of being rather sleepy. However, there were inns on the road that catered to those who preferred a certain lifestyle, and he knew just the one. Miles rubbed a hand across his face. It had been some time since he'd set foot in such places and he had rather hoped he would never have to again.

"For Augusta," he murmured to himself.

Once his horse was saddled, he rode out into the next county, crossing the border between Hampshire and West Sussex. A mile down the road, he came across the traveler's inn. He sucked in a breath and led his horse through the carriage entrance and into the stables. For an inn frequented by those on the road to the coast, the stables could always be relied upon to have fresh water and feed for the horses as well as hardworking groomsmen. It was not to cater to travelers, however. No, the Bell Inn preferred richer clientele who had plenty of cash to lose—be it to gambling or to whores.

It had been years since he'd been to the place. Miles could safely say this place had been the start of his downfall into a life far from that of a gentleman. He could blame the pressure from his parents or how dull he found London society or even his privileged upbringing for protecting him from such places but the fact was, he'd been a fool. Worse than that, he'd been thoughtless and selfish, not caring how his behavior might impact others. Places like the Bell Inn had become home and he'd wasted plenty of money and time drinking and gaming.

Tugging at his cravat as it seemed to tighten around his throat, he ducked into the rear entranceway of the whitewashed building. Mud and boot prints marred the lower halves of the interior walls. Evidence of fights revealed itself in fist-sized holes in some of the wooden paneling that lined the wall to the right—a brief reminder of the inn's ancient history. The light was low, lanterns and candles lit few and far between while the shutters on the windows were half-closed—deliberately so unsuspecting patrons would be more vulnerable to pickpockets or someone cheating at cards. The inn employed several people to help with such matters, ensuring they received a cut of any ill-gotten gains.

Smoke lingered around the rafters. Miles ducked under several of the uneven beams as he made his way to the bar. Ancient buildings like this were never designed to accommodate someone of his size and stature. He allowed himself a grim smile.

He recalled the first time he'd entered this building as a young man. His size and strength had always made him feel invulnerable and he felt like he owned the world when he came across this place. Men from all walks of life wished to come to know him. Of course, a lot of that was to do with how useful his fists could be and the fact he was heir to his father's fortune and title. He hadn't much cared at the time. These people were far more interesting than anybody could find at White's or Almack's.

He rested an elbow on the bar, relieved that the barkeep was not one who would recognize him. Many of the faces here were different, though he spotted a few from his time here—Beth, a prostitute known for her flexibility who had aged dramatically in the past years, her once red hair washed out into a premature pinkish white. Fat Giles was here too, a man with an eye for cards who no one could ever beat. Miles had suspected he cheated but had never been able to prove it. He remained hunched over in his usual corner, chewing on the corner of his lip—a fake tell used to deceive others. His face had always been grisly, pockmarked from measles, and now red and creased from too much alcohol. The additional years had done little to improve his looks.

The diminutive barkeep peered up at him, his expression bored. Wiry and a good five years younger than himself, the lad seemed too sober and clean to work at a place like this.

"What can I get you?"

"An ale." Miles slid a coin over the counter. "And information."

The lad folded his arms and stared at Miles. Miles chuckled. The barkeep might not seem at home but he certainly already knew how things worked around here. Miles added two more coins.

"An ale it is." The lad poured the drink into a battered tankard that had likely been smashed around someone's head at some point. He pushed it across the bar toward Miles and waited for him to take a sip.

"What do you need?"

"A man called Jenkins. Rich chap, well-dressed, with fair hair. Have you seen him?"

"We get plenty of rich chaps here, believe it or not."

"I believe it."

The barkeep leaned back against the bar behind him. "What's his poison?"

"Probably the women, though I think he'd be free with his money. He'll bring a crowd with him. Had a penchant for...group activities."

"Oh, that pervert. I know him." He unfolded his arms and straightened. "I ain't seen him today but he was here yesterday and will probably be here on Saturday. He favors Sweet Lilly and she'll be visiting that night."

Miles nodded. Four days' time. In the meantime, he would have to keep an eye out for Jenkins. If the man attended anymore local events, he'd use it as a good opportunity to do some more damage to Augusta's reputation. He did not much want to throw about any threats at a garden party or dinner event but he'd do what he must.

However, come Saturday and he'd have Jenkins precisely where he wanted him. For once, Miles's rough past might prove useful. If there was one thing he knew how to do, it was to scare a man half to death. Jenkins would sorely regret ever harming Augusta's reputation.

Chapter Eleven

"GUS GUS!"

Augusta grimaced. She was in no mood for talk of weddings or Henry's return.

She stilled her grooming of Bella, a beautiful sable mare who had only been with them for a few months but already had the markings of a loyal and sweet horse. Oh Lord, what if her mother had heard of these rumors?

No, she sounded far too cheery for that and there would be no use of 'Gus Gus' if that were the case. It was more likely to be Augusta Elizabeth Charlotte Snow if she were in trouble.

She resumed her grooming of Bella, cooing to her while she ran the brush over her coat. "It's so much nicer to be here with you, Bella," she murmured. "Why did I ever think it would be wise to try to become adored?"

Her plans to show Henry just what he was missing had been a complete failure. She had opened herself up to derision from people she did not even like...not to mention what had happened between her and Miles. She could not help but think if she had just remained a wallflower, none of this would have occurred. Miles would not have kissed her and she would not feel as though she were tangled in a web of her own making, powerless to escape, powerless to make a change.

Powerless to avoid the agony of knowing she had kissed Lord Miles Ashwick and would never be able to forget it—even if *he* could.

"Gus, Gus, there you are! I should have known."

Twisting to view her mother in the door of the stables, Augusta winced at the bright daylight that streamed in around her, highlighting her petite figure. Her mother stepped into the gloom of the stables and wrinkled her nose. "Miles is here to see you." Mama pressed her hands together. "No doubt to discuss Henry's return. You had better hurry. It would not do to keep him waiting." She glanced over her with a sigh. "At least Henry will not see you like this."

Augusta grimaced. She was dirty and likely a little smelly too. "Perhaps I should change..."

"No, no, no." Her mother waved her hands at her. "He has been waiting for you long enough."

Sighing, Augusta nodded and lowered the brush. She swept her hands over her straw laden skirts and tucked a few loose strands of hair back into their pins as they walked back to the house. Her mother indicated into the parlor room and murmured, "I will be in the breakfast room," before backing away.

Why her mother thought she needed privacy with Miles, she did not know, but she could not decide whether to be grateful or not. At least then if Miles had something to say about these rumors, her mother would be unaware, but it would be much easier to remain proper with her mother present. Perhaps she might even forget that she kissed him and could not help but relive the moment over and over whenever she was alone.

Alas, she could hardly ask her mother to remain for such reasons.

Drawing her shoulders straight, she entered the drawing room. Miles struck a masculine feature against the pale blues and silvers of the room. Hands clasped behind his back, he stood straight, eyeing a painting of a battle at sea. He turned when one of the floorboards creaked beneath her feet and his lips curved.

"It seems those horses warrant more attention than I do."

"I came as soon as my mother informed me you were here." She pressed clammy hands down her skirts, wishing she'd changed. "Thank you for ensuring I'm thoroughly aware of my unkempt state."

His smile broadened. "If it helps, I rather like you in this state. Straw suits you better than flowers or feathers." He closed the gap between them, so swiftly that her heart nearly jumped out of her chest. He reached for her and she froze. Was he going to kiss her? Embrace her? When her mother was in the next room and the doors were wide open?

He tugged something from her hair and brandished it in front of her. She let herself sag a little. Hay. A mere strand of hay.

He twisted it in his fingers, eyeing it. "A rare thing that a woman can look more beautiful coming straight from the stables," he mused.

Augusta felt the blush in her cheeks. "Why do you have to say such things?" she murmured.

"I thought all women liked to be called beautiful."

"When you say things like that it makes it hard to..." Oh Lord, what was she admitting? She stepped away and went to the window, letting the slight breeze that stole through the open window cool her heated face. "What was it you wished to speak of?" She kept her gaze on the gardens but hardly saw a thing, too aware of his large presence growing near.

He had to be a few feet from her—enough to be perfectly proper—but the hairs on the back of her neck tingled. Miles remained silent long enough for her to be forced to turn around.

"Miles?"

For the briefest of moments, there was something soft in his intense gaze. It vanished quickly behind that constant quizzical look, as though he was forever trying to hide some part of him. Sometimes she wondered if that was why he teased her so—because he feared her seeing whatever was underneath.

"Jenkins was behind the rumors."

Augusta pressed a hand to her stomach. "For certain?"

"I have yet to...speak with the man but I am certain enough."

"Oh Lord." She sank onto the nearest chair and placed her head in her hands. "This is all my fault."

"Gus..."

"It is." She lifted her head. "You warned me but I was determined. I thought I could prove something to Henry...to myself. What a fool I was."

"You wanted to prove something to Henry?"

Pressing fingers to her temples, she nodded grimly. Now Miles would think her even more silly.

"I was tired of waiting. I thought if I showed that I was not just a meek wallflower, then..." She shrugged. "I don't know. Then maybe he would hear and return for me, and maybe I would not feel so boring and dull and like I was cast aside."

Miles chuckled.

She pursed her lips. "This amuses you?"

"Only that you could think yourself boring and dull."

"I am certain that is almost the definition of a wallflower and you cannot deny that I have become one."

"Gus, you are far from dull, believe me. And I have seen and met many unusual people in my life. In our circles, there are plenty of the same people. They talk the same, behave the same, repeat the same amusements over and over. You are absolutely nothing like them."

Augusta blinked at him. His words were so impassioned that she almost believed him. "If I am so fascinating, why did Henry leave me?"

"That will be for him to explain but I can only say this, my brother was a fool not to marry you as soon as he had proposed. If it had been me—" He stilled and snapped his mouth shut.

His gaze darkened and a rush of excitement swelled in her chest. She slowly rose and took two steps toward him. He remained frozen, creases between his brows forming as though he was in pain. She was terrified, every limb feeling weak, her heart thudding in her ears like a war drum, yet she could not help herself from saying it. "If it had been you...?"

His expression grew more pained. No hint of that sardonic smile or the creases around his eyes remained. "Gus..." His voice was husky.

She should say it. Just admit it all and throw caution to the wind. Tell him she did not wish to marry Henry and that she...she...well, she wanted more from him. But the words remained trapped. Apparently her courage would only take her so far.

"Gus," he repeated, reaching for her.

She glanced only briefly at the open doorway but she could not say with honesty whether she could have cared if they were in full view of everyone. Rising onto tiptoes, she flung her arms around his neck and flattened her lips to his. A groan rumbled up from within him and he held her close, tightly, as though he was fearful she might pull away.

As if she could.

His mouth upon hers, his firm, warm lips—they kept her captive. This was even better than that night at his house. There was no shock or surprise...just pleasure. She angled her head and gave him access, allowing his tongue to sweep over hers. The world around her blurred and he bundled her closer, lifting her from the ground. He kissed her again and again, taking more and more from her but giving back so much. She could have sworn she could kiss this man for eternity. Pleasure swept through her at the feeling of his firm body against hers, his strong arms enveloping her.

He lowered her back to the ground, easing his hold but moving his mouth across her face and down her neck. She arched into the ecstasy, tingles racing from every spot of skin that he kissed.

"Gus," he murmured, running his hands up and down her back.

A delicate cough from the other room splintered the moment. Augusta froze in his arms and he straightened. They didn't break apart, and for that, she was grateful as she was not certain she would remain standing. Drawing in a long breath, she turned her head toward the doorway then let her head sag against his chest. Her mother remained in the breakfast room and remained oblivious.

Miles moved his hands to her shoulders and eased her back. "That was rather reckless."

Too aware of her ragged breaths and heated cheeks, she kept her head lowered as she nodded.

"I did not come here to do that," he said.

She lifted her head, spotting that sardonic smile back in place. "I did not think you did."

"You're a secret temptress, Gus."

"I am not," she protested in a harsh whisper.

"I know." He shoved a hand through his hair. "It is my fault as usual. I forget how to behave as a gentleman around you it seems. I shall have to beg forgiveness once more."

"But..." What if she did not wish to give it? What if she knew she was as much to blame as he was? The first kiss, perhaps, could have been entirely on him, but this one...this one was not.

Her courage was gone, though. Swept away by the madness of the moment. If there was ever a time to tell him how she felt, it was now, but she could hardly comprehend it herself yet. A few months ago, she had been pining for Henry. Now she could think of nothing else other than kissing Miles.

"I shall have to work hard for that forgiveness, I see."

"No," she blurted out. "No, that is not what—"

"I think it best I leave you now." He retrieved his hat from a nearby table and put it on. "And while I might not be the best of gentlemen, I shall see to it that Jenkins ceases his gossip, I promise that much."

Twining her hands in front of her, she nodded. He dipped his head then left the room. She heard murmurs of him conversing with her mother but could not make out the words. At least her mother would have little idea what had just occurred.

She almost envied her mother. If only she could be in ignorance too. Expunge what had happened from her mind and move on with her life. Miles appeared to have no difficulties in doing so. She sank back onto the chair and touched her still tingling lips. If only she was still that naive, excited girl who could not wait to marry Henry.

But she had changed. Time had changed her. *Miles* had changed her.

So what was she going to do about it?

Chapter Twelve

MILES RELEASED THE tension from the bow and dropped the arrow to the ground when he recognized the man approaching. It had taken a moment as his usual chestnut hair had lightened, flashes of gold streaked through it, and his skin was darker than usual. Henry's broad smile appeared whiter against the tan of his skin. Miles curled his fingers around the bow. He was happy his brother was home—really he was.

But there was no running from it now.

Henry was here to marry Augusta.

His heart gave a sickly thud against his chest and he drew in a long breath through his nostrils in an attempt to govern it. He would not allow his foolish emotions to govern him any longer. He'd already proved himself entirely incapable of managing them yet again.

Henry strode rapidly over to where Miles had been practicing and jerked his head toward the target. "Still room for improvement I see."

Miles lifted a brow. "Almost all of them at dead center."

"I could still best you," his brother challenged.

"We shall see."

Henry's grin widened and he embraced Miles before stepping back. "It is good to see you, Brother. It appears the years have done you no favors."

"Whereas they have done you plenty. I imagine all the woman will enjoy your new exotic look."

"With the unpredictable summers we enjoy here in England, I suspect I shall be back to pale and uninteresting before long."

Miles shook his head. Henry had always been known as the more dashing one. Up until deserting them all in favor of travelling, he'd been an exemplary man. Charming, a gentleman to the core, traditionally attractive, and with the sort of personality that drew people to him, Miles could not deny envying his brother many a time. Though, none more so than now. Henry would finally claim Augusta as his.

"You must be tired," Miles said, propping the bow against the target and loosening the arm guard from his wrist before tucking it in his pocket.

"I have enjoyed better journeys, but I have also endured worse."

"I can imagine." Miles nodded. "You shall have to avail me of your adventures."

"I will indeed. Though, first, if we may, refreshments. I am parched and the journey from Southampton in the mail coach was longer than anticipated. The bloody thing threw a wheel."

"Of course." Miles motioned toward the house. "Let us get you inside."

Henry peered up at the house from their position on the flat grass that spanned one side of the lake. "It is good to be home."

Miles peered at him. "Is it?"

"Absolutely. Why would it not be?"

"Because, dear Brother, Mother and I have been writing to you for quite some time in attempts to persuade you home."

Henry grimaced. "I know."

They began their walk back toward the house, climbing up the gentle slope that led into the formal gardens. Once between the lines of planted flowers and carefully trimmed, waist-height trees, Henry paused and glanced around. "It really is good to be home. I missed the green of England. There is none quite like it."

"I would not know," Miles murmured. He had travelled somewhat in his younger years but only to the nearest reaches of Europe. His younger brother was no doubt far more experienced than him at this point. Travel did not appeal greatly to Miles but he could not help experience another pang of envy. Sometimes, he wished he didn't love Henry so damned much. It would make life a lot easier.

"I understand why you would not be happy with me, Miles," Henry announced as they followed the path that led around the house to the rear doors.

"I never said that."

Henry lifted a shoulder. "You did not need to. I would not be happy with me. I abandoned you to deal with all that you had inherited, I abandoned Mother in her time of grief and...well..." Henry glanced down. "I abandoned my commitments."

His heart gave another untimely thud. "Augusta," he muttered.

Henry nodded. "It was not my finest moment. Nor can I claim these past years were."

"She has been patient indeed."

Miles stepped aside so Henry could enter the glass doors that led into the ballroom. Henry paused just inside the threshold and stared up at the ceilings. He smiled. "Things have not changed one jot." He looked to Miles. "It seems you are doing a fine job indeed."

Miles merely lifted his shoulders and followed Henry over to the large fireplace that was rarely lit. Henry paused here, tracing a finger over the carved wood of the surround.

"Henry?" Miles prompted. It was rare to see his brother so introspective or for him to be this damned quiet. He'd half-expected to have to endure endless tales of his adventuring.

Henry glanced at him, his blue eyes filled with a strange sadness that made Miles regret every thought of annoyance or anger directed toward him. He smiled briefly and straightened. "I know I have been remiss in neglecting you all."

"You said that, Henry, you do not—"

His brother held up a hand. "I was not in the best frame of mind when Father died." He sighed. "And I know it was a shock to us all. He had always seemed so healthy and vital, as though he might live forever."

Miles nodded. Their father's death had come as a shock to them all. He had certainly not been prepared to take on the mantle of viscount and all the responsibilities it had come with. The only thing he could be grateful for was it prevented him from ever sinking back into his old ways.

"It is a terrible excuse, particularly when, from what I hear, you are doing a stellar job of filling his shoes."

Miles said nothing.

"And, of course, I leaped headlong into proposing to Augusta."

Clenching his jaw, Miles stared sightlessly into the empty fireplace.

"She certainly deserved better." Henry rubbed a hand over his face. "But we were always going to be together, were we not? It was what everyone wanted and, well, it's Augusta...she's a fine girl and we all knew she'd make a fine wife."

Miles ground his teeth together, only stopping when his jaw hurt.

"It just seemed the right thing to do," Henry said. "Life was short and people could vanish at any moment."

"And the fleeing the country part?"

"Not my finest moment, I'll admit."

"You do not seem to have done poorly for it."

Henry's brow lifted. "You are angry at me?"

Miles pressed his lips together. "You did leave us all rather in the lurch, Henry."

"And I left you fending for me with regards to Augusta." Henry sighed. "I know I have much to make up for."

"That is why you have returned?" Miles frowned. Though he looked healthier and more worldly, there were creases around his brother's eyes that had not been there before. It could be that the sun was to blame but something seemed to weigh on his brother's shoulders and he was not certain it was simply guilt.

"When I was in Hungary, there was a mudslide." He gave a shudder. "Awful thing it was. Lots of deaths."

"A mudslide?" Miles echoed.

Henry nodded. "I was lucky. The building in which I had been staying in was washed away. But I had found this woman trapped and was trying to aid her. Because of her, I was not where I should have been."

"Christ."

Henry gave a grim smile. "It rather put a damper on all of my travels, and it made me realize—"

"Henry!" Their mother hastened into the ballroom and picked up pace when she spotted Henry. Flinging her arms around him, her weight nearly sent him toppling back against the fireplace. "I heard you were spotted approaching but I did not really believe it." She drew back and pressed hands to either side of his face.

Miles could not help smile at his mother's beatific expression. It was no secret that Henry had always been her 'baby' and as much his brother had bemoaned his treatment as the youngest, he knew Henry enjoyed the close relationship he had with her.

"Goodness, you do look brown. And older." She stepped back. "But quite regal because of it. Do you not think, Miles?"

Miles smirked at his brother's expression. "Oh, yes, regal indeed."

"Come, we must get you some food and drink. No doubt you are in need of it." Their mother looped her arm through Henry's and forcibly dragged him out of the ballroom and down the corridor to the second drawing room. Miles followed, half-listening to his mother's incessant questions of the journey. It was good to have Henry back in a way. His mother had missed him and there was something odd about occupying this house without his brother. But, of course, it meant, he assumed, the wedding would be going ahead.

Unless Henry was looking to call it off. Augusta would be ruined, if so, but perhaps they would be able to...

"Miles?"

"Yes?" He looked to his mother.

"I was just saying we should hold a ball to celebrate Henry's return."

Miles grimaced and ignored his brother's amused expression. He'd done enough hosting and enough balls of late. "Perhaps," he murmured.

Mother pulled the bell and practically dragged Henry over to the sofa, tugging on his arm so that he practically fell into his seat. "You must tell me of all your adventures."

"I will of course regale you with all my tales, Mother," Henry promised, "but first you must tell me of you. And Miles. I see you are both looking well, but what has my brother been up to of late? You know how closed-mouthed he is."

Miles glowered at his brother. If he was digging for any tales of misbehavior, there would be none. It had been a long time since he'd done anything disreputable and he'd wished Henry would remember that. If anyone had been—

"Miles has been doing wonderfully. I know your father would be so proud, God rest his soul."

Henry shot Miles a smug look. "Good to hear it."

Miles narrowed his gaze at him and Henry chuckled. "His sense of humor has not improved in my time away it seems."

Rolling his eyes, Miles reached for a biscuit and shoved it whole into his mouth.

"Nor has his manners," their mother declared.

"I have perfectly good manners," Miles protested around a mouthful of crumbs.

"Try telling that to the rug," Henry said, casting his gaze pointedly down to where a sprinkling of crumbs had landed.

Miles grunted and leaned back in the armchair. "To think there were times when I missed you."

"I have no doubt you did, Brother." Henry grinned. "But all is well now. Your little brother is here to keep you company."

"I like my own company," Miles muttered.

"I really do think—" Their mother paused and frowned. "Goodness, I just realized I was to visit with Mrs. Lowbury today. I had better have word sent. Perhaps she can come here and see how Henry is doing. Oh, she will be most delighted to see him." She rose as swiftly as she could from the seat, straightening her skirts and twisting briefly to clasp her hands around Henry's face. "How handsome you are and how wonderful it is to have you home."

Miles waited until she had left the room before leaning forward, his elbows upon his knees. "You have made Mother's day. No, make that year."

"I am glad." Henry pressed a hand to his mouth. "And I am gladdened that you are not angry with me."

"Angry?"

"Come on, Miles. I know you. None of this would have been easy on you—looking after mother, taking over the estate...even looking after Augusta..."

"Well, I have only really spent time with her recently..." Too much time, in far too close confines, in a far too familiar way. But he could not admit to that.

"Anyway, what I was trying to say about the mudslide..."

"Do not tell mother of that. She'll have a fainting fit."

"I have no intention of uttering a word to her." Henry lifted a cup and took a long sip of tea. "But in a way, it was a good thing that happened to me. It reminded me once again that life is short and that running away from my responsibilities was not a fine way to spend it."

"So you are returned for good?"

Henry nodded. "Indeed. And I intend to make things up to you. To you and Augusta. I shall be here to help with anything you need. Put me to work. If travelling taught me anything, it was how to labor."

"I will certainly not refuse any aid from you, Henry."

"Excellent." He finished the cup of tea before setting it on the tray in the middle of the table. "But before I do anything, I must speak with Augusta. It is high time we set a date."

Miles had known it was coming. Maybe he'd been in denial, believing that Henry might in fact want to break things off. It didn't matter though. It still struck him like ten rounds to the gut. He drew in a breath and forced his expression to remain neutral.

"You still wish to marry her then," he said.

"Of course. After all, I made the girl a promise, and what sort of a gentleman would I be if I just broke it off after making her wait for so damned long?" Henry paused, a crease appearing between his brows. "Unless you can think of a reason that I should not."

Miles shook his head slowly. "No, no reason at all." He forced a painful smile. "No doubt, Augusta will be thrilled to hear you say such a thing."

"Excellent. With any luck, she shall forgive me quickly enough for my absence when I make quick with setting a date."

"No doubt she will," he agreed.

Because Augusta was too damned good for either of them.

Chapter Thirteen

"GOODNESS, HE HAS GROWN handsome!"

Augusta looked up from her embroidery, having been entirely unaware that her mother was in the parlor room until her squeaky exclamation. Hands clasped to her face, her mother bounced up and down on her toes while peering out of the window.

"So handsome," she repeated before turning to Augusta. "Perhaps these years apart were not so very bad. He was fine-looking before but to see him now..." She gestured rapidly with her hands. "Come and steal a look, quickly, before he reaches the house."

Augusta swallowed the knot in her throat. It had to be Henry. There was no one else from whom she had spent years apart or who her mother would gush over. "It's fine, Mama, I am sure I shall see him in just a moment unless he is here to see Papa."

Part of her hoped that would be the case. Perhaps he was intending to break things off. It would be disastrous, of course, and her family would be heartbroken but at least then...well, at least then she would have the decision made for her even if it left her alone and eventually destitute.

She grimaced at her rather poorly stitched rendition of a violet. Normally embroidery brought her a sense of peace, but the past few weeks, she had been unable to concentrate thanks to Miles. She sighed. Destitution was hardly a fate she would meet with relish and she was being foolish. Miles would not save her. He clearly regretted kissing her.

"Stand up, Gus. You need to straighten your skirts." Her mother grabbed her embroidery from her hand and flung it carelessly onto the sofa then snatched her hands and hauled her to her feet. Fingers pinched at her cheeks then spread over her waist and down then fluttered over her hair, pressing the pins more tightly into her head.

Augusta winced as pins jabbed her scalp and batted her mother's invasive hands away. "Ouch, Mama!"

"Thank goodness you are wearing one of your new gowns. What a fine thing it was you decided to finally take me up on my offer."

Augusta rather enjoyed her new gowns, she had to admit. Not because of the attention they brought her but they certainly flattered her non-descript figure better and brought out color in her cheeks. At least if she had to face Henry, she could do so with a little more pride than previously.

A knock at the door and Mrs. Goldsmith entering made Augusta's mouth dry. "Lord Henry here for you, ma'am," the housekeeper said.

"Please show him in," her mother said, clasping her hands delicately in front of her and adopting a smile that made Augusta raise her brow.

She tried to do the same but it felt odd on her lips, as though it should not be there, and she could feel that it did not reach her eyes. A pang of nerves fluttered hard in her breast, begging to escape or to be gulped down with fresh air. Her feet twitched at the sound of heavy, masculine footsteps.

It was no lie. Henry had certainly grown more handsome. He beamed at them both as though he had missed them greatly. Augusta remembered that smile and how it had made her feel like the most important woman on earth. Dressed in hessians and a finely cut jacket and waistcoat, the dark blue emphasized the tan color of his skin. He seemed older and wiser but the years and exotic countries had certainly done him many favors.

"Henry, how wonderful it is to see you!" her mother declared. "And looking so well too. Have you been returned long?"

"But a day," he said.

"Goodness and we were your first visit? How kind you are." She motioned to the chair. "Will you not sit?"

"I was hoping I might take Augusta for a short walk. We will not go far but I have a hankering to see the fields around here again. I have missed all the English scenery so very much." His gaze landed on Augusta. "Although, there is some quite pleasant scenery in here too."

Augusta glanced to her feet. She was not unused to Henry's flattery but he had always had the ability to flatter anyone, whether they were deserving of it or not. However, this time it seemed genuine.

"A fine idea, especially with the lovely weather we are having," her mother enthused. "Do go now before it all changes its mind and decides to shower upon us."

"Mama," Augusta protested as she practically shoved Augusta out of the door.

Once they were outside the house and Augusta had retrieved a bonnet, Augusta drew in a long gulp of fresh air but it did not dispel the coiling tension that was slowly wrapping itself around her heart and lungs. Henry motioned along the road that led away from her family home. "Shall we?"

She nodded and tightened the ribbons around her face, grateful for the slight protection the brim gave her from Henry.

"You are looking well indeed, Augusta."

She kept her gaze ahead. "As do you, Henry."

"The time apart has done you well."

"Thank you."

He paused, forcing her to face him. Although his hair had lightened and his skin was darker, she saw the old Henry still there. The one who could charm anyone, and make her laugh with his easy wit, and talk until she no longer felt shy. She understood now, why she had been willing to wait so long for him. He had always been a catch and still was.

"I understand if you are angry with me, Augusta."

She opened her mouth and closed it. As wonderful as Henry was, he had never been one for introspection or apologies.

"I have treated you poorly and I will have to beg your forgiveness for that."

Her heart panged as she recalled another person who wanted her forgiveness. Why they all thought it was so hard to gain from her, she did not know. She never considered she might have any power over anyone so why would she not grant it easily?

"Henry, you do not—"

He held up a hand. "I was immature and in an ill frame of mind. However, I am returned for good, and I should like to make good on my promise to you."

She felt the breath trap in her lungs. How many times had she imagined him returning for her? Telling her that all was well and they would marry? There had been various scenarios, including him taking her into his arms and kissing her breathlessly or perhaps her flinging her arms around him and being so bold as to kiss him.

Her arms felt leaden and he made no approach. She was somewhat grateful for his caution. After all, she had been kissing his brother only days ago. She regretted he was being so pleasant and kind. It would make it a lot easier to feel no guilt over what she had done with Miles if he had no apologies to make.

"If you feel you have it in you to forgive me, I should like to set a date soon. We shall have to marry locally—there will be no big event—but I suspect you would prefer that."

She smiled vaguely. Henry knew her to an extent—understood her shyness and dislike of attention. She should not be surprised by that. After all, they had spent many days together throughout their lives.

"I would prefer that," she agreed.

"Excellent. Shall we walk some more?" he suggested. "I was not lying about wishing to see the lands around your house. They hold a great many good memories for me."

"Please."

They strolled along the road then followed the worn line that cut through the grass and would lead toward his family's estate.

"I imagine you have seen some quite exotic landscapes on your adventures," she commented.

"Indeed, though there is something about England's gentle beauty that I missed."

"You shall have to regale me of your travels."

"I will. And you must promise to tell me all with which you've been occupied."

Augusta swallowed. Her time had been filled with horses, embroidery, tiresome socials events, and...and, well, kissing Miles. Good lord, what a terrible person she was. Henry should never have abandoned her for so long but that did not justify her own behavior. She exhaled slowly.

"Henry, I—"

"I should like for us to start again, Augusta." He paused by the brow of the slope that led down toward the Charlecote estate. From here, they could see the tips of the house, its elegant adornments peeking up over the land. She could not help wonder if Miles was home.

Was he thinking of her?

No, of course not. He likely wished to push her from his mind just as she did him. For him, it was probably easy enough.

She turned to Henry. "I...I fear I have not been as...as loyal a fiancée as I should have been."

Henry's lips curved. "Whatever you have done, Augusta, my sins are far worse. I should never have left you for so long. It is my hope that we can forget these years and go on as we intended. I think we are a good match, you and I. We have always had a good time together, have we not?"

She nodded, biting down on her bottom lip. Henry likely did not realize quite what she meant about her disloyalty. After all, no one would expect that quiet Miss Augusta Snow might kiss another man!

But he was right. They were a good match. They had known each other for a long time and Henry's easy manner always seemed to bring her out of her shell. Whenever they attended balls and the like, she knew Henry would take the attention for her, allowing her to slip back into being a wallflower with ease. She doubted they would ever argue and despite Henry's absence, he was no bad man. There were far too many husbands out there who were willing to lay a hand on their wives or ignore them once they had borne them a child.

If she married Henry, she would be safe, and content.

And she would have no choice but to forget she had ever had any feelings for Miles.

"So what do you say? Shall we set a date?" He took her hand and eased off her glove, keeping hold of it in one hand while his gloved fingers held her own. It was the sort of moment she had dreamed of not so long ago.

She focused hard on drawing pleasure from the moment, in looking into blue eyes whose beauty she had once thought could never be beaten by anyone else's. She absorbed the feeling of his strong hand upon hers and tried to find the tingle that should arise and send the tiny hairs on her arms standing on end. He dropped his lips to the back of her hand, brushing them briefly over her knuckles. They were warm and soft but there were no tingles.

He straightened and grinned. “If you wish to make me wait, I would not hold it against you.”

She glanced to the house, imagining Miles sitting in his drawing room then looked back to Henry, his strong features highlighted by the afternoon sun. This was real. This was within reach. “I would not make you wait,” she finally said. “Let us set a date.”

Chapter Fourteen

A LIGHT SHOWER SPLIT the sky as Miles approached the inn. It pattered on the brim of his hat but brought welcome relief from what had turned into an evening thick with heat. Puddles built quickly in the ruts etched into the ground, the dry, cracked mud not yet ready to absorb the moisture. Miles handed his horse over to a groom and stepped around several patches of water before ducking into the inn.

The evening heat made the taproom even less inviting than previously, bringing with it the scent of stale and fresh sweat. The beer was warm too and Miles sipped it slowly from his position by the bar. He remained standing but kept his elbows propped on the chipped wood, remaining stooped over and hopefully avoiding any attention.

Unfortunately, his height and breadth frequently caught people's eye. It was what had started him down the path of an unsavory lifestyle for a soon-to-be-lord after all.

He peered surreptitiously around as he nursed the ale, looking for any sign of Jenkins. Now, more than ever, it was vital for Miles to ensure Jenkins did nothing to ruin Augusta's happiness. From what his brother had said, she had seemed pleased to set a date. He tightened his grip on the handle of the pewter tankard then forced himself to release it. He was happy for her—really he was. Nothing mattered more than if she was happy.

But he'd be damned if he didn't wish he was the man to do it.

Still, it seemed Henry's revelation had changed his brother's attitude and would ensure that he made a good husband. They were the better match, there was no denying it. Someone sweet and shy like Augusta would bloom under Henry's guidance.

So absorbed was he in torturing himself with thoughts of Augusta and his brother together that he didn't notice the arrival of Jenkins until the man was seated around a table with several friends and a pretty, mature woman was draped across his lap. She leaned in every few minutes while cards were dealt across the table and whispered things in Jenkins' ears that were either amusing or filthy. He suspected the latter from Jenkins' salacious grin.

Miles scanned the room surreptitiously. Jenkins had three friends with him—no doubt enjoying the idea of 'slumming it'. Jenkins was no weak man but nor was he a match for Miles. His three friends were of average build and none looked as though they had any fighting experience.

Not that Miles was hoping for a fight—his fighting days were behind him—but in a place like this, it was easy for an altercation to turn into a brawl. He flexed his hands and opted to wait. With any luck, he could catch Jenkins alone, issue a few threats, and be done with the man. Miles ordered another ale—this time warmer than the last.

The summer sun took time to set, dripping its amber warmth through the murky windows of the inn and reminding

Miles of his time spent waiting. He drained another ale and motioned for one more. The weak liquid did little to affect him but he'd stopped noticing how warm it was or the sediment lurking in the bottom of his tankard by such a poorly brewed drink.

Jenkins had left the table but once and accompanied by two of his friends who apparently shadowed his every move. Miles knew few of the 'new money' set but whoever they were, they likely owned less than Jenkins, hence what appeared to be an unhealthy dose of hero-worshipping the man. Miles could not deny there were those who behaved like that toward him thanks to his title and wealth but Jenkins was happy to take advantage of the devotion whereas Miles preferred to avoid it. No decent friendship could be carved from such a relationship.

He remained hunched low and Jenkins was too involved in cards to notice. He lost money easily and with little care. Miles shook his head to himself. He'd been there once before but he did not approach losing money as a great pastime. He'd made wins—big ones—and that had made him hungry for more. It would be easy, he thought, to prove himself—to add to the coffers of the family. But the cards were a false mistress and he was soon losing anything he'd gained. His gambling had also drawn the attention of a crowd of people he'd have been better off not knowing. Miles deeply regretted ever touching those cards and he suspected Jenkins might feel the same one day.

Regardless of what might happen to the man eventually, however, Miles had to deal with him today. He could not wait for inevitable fate to intervene and show him the error of his ways. Jenkins finally moved from the table to use the outhouse and Miles followed at a slight distance. He waited under the eaves of the inn until Jenkins was finished and he hurried back through the rain toward the taproom. Miles stepped in front of him, blocking his entrance.

"Damn you, I'm getting wet." Jenkins lifted his gaze and a smirk quirked his lips. "Ashwick, I never expected to find you at a place like this."

"I am not here by choice."

"Well, then you had better get going. Now, if you do not mind..." He tried to step around Miles but Miles moved in front of him again.

"I need a word, Jenkins."

"And you may have it, but, pray, can we have it inside? This moleskin does not do well in rain."

Miles shook his head and snatched Jenkins by the collar of his coat, hauling him away from the entrance to the recesses at the entrance to the stables.

"Ashwick, I know you are fond of your fists but there really is no need for brutality." Jenkins tore his jacket from Miles's hand, his amused expression distorting. "I had heard you were rather a brute back in the day. I had not realized it was true until you threw that punch."

Miles ground his teeth together. He supposed it was only a matter of time before Jenkins heard tales of his exploits now that he was spending time in such places. Some of Miles's acquaintances understood he'd been rather a 'naughty boy' when he was younger but did not wish to delve any further. He preferred it that way.

"I'm not here to talk about whether I can throw a punch or not," Miles said tightly, keeping his stance as threatening as possible. "I'm here to put a stop to these rumors you have been spreading."

Jenkins's lips curled. "Rumors? My dear fellow, you should know better than anyone that there are always rumors amongst high society."

"I know for a fact these come from you."

"And what rumors might these be?"

Damn the man, he was going to make him say it aloud. "About Miss Snow."

"The delectable Miss Snow..."

Miles fisted his hands and forced a hot breath through his nostrils as he willed himself to remain calm. He had not come here to fall back into old patterns. All he wanted to do was protect Augusta.

"You say another word about her, and you will regret it, Jenkins."

"I cannot help it if people make assumptions." He shrugged. "It is strange for people to see this little wallflower bloom while her fiancé's brother stalks her every step." He cocked his head. "I congratulate you on noticing her so quickly. I'll admit it took me a little while but you found quite a treasure there."

"I swear to God, Jenkins, you're begging me to hit you," he said through gritted teeth.

"Do it." Jenkins folded his arms. "You titled folk think you are something special because you've clung onto your money for so long but I'd love to see the man beneath all the shine."

Miles chuckled. "If you think attacking my money or my title will bother me, you need to find another rung to cling to."

"Miss Snow bothers you, though. Not that I can blame you. I did rather fancy getting between her thighs before your bro—"

Miles felt the give of flesh before he'd registered what he'd done. Jenkins doubled over and fought to draw in breaths. Miles's knuckles throbbed slightly and he kept his hand fisted while heat roared through him. "You have no right to speak of Miss Snow," Miles hissed.

Jenkins lifted his head. "And...you...do...?" he gasped.

"More right than you." He put a hand to Jenkins's shoulder, forcing him up against the wall. "You leave Miss Snow alone or I will show you how dark my past really was."

Jenkins's gaze flickered and a tiny smile dared to quirk on his lips before vanishing. "I will," he rasped.

Miles searched his gaze then stepped back, allowing Jenkins to drop down to his knees. He drew in a breath of cooling air and looked up briefly, letting the raindrops spatter over his heated skin.

"Just so long as *you* do," he heard Jenkins mutter as Miles stepped away.

He stilled. Jenkins was the sort of man who was determined to have the last word. He'd probably let himself be beaten to a bloody pulp and still be spitting insults. The man wasn't worth it. Miles flexed his fist and eyed the door of the tavern. He hadn't wanted to use threats. Hadn't wanted to unleash his anger. It reminded him too much of who he'd once been.

He sighed. He needed a damned drink and no weak ale this time.

Ducking back into the inn, he ordered a whisky.

"Still throwing punches I see?"

Miles glanced at the man who approached him from the side. Damn it. There was no way this whiskey was worth it. "Nester," Miles said in greeting then turned his focus back onto his drink, draining it quickly and slamming the glass down.

"Haven't seen you around here for a long time."

"For good reason." Miles stood but Nester put a hand to his arm. The man had aged significantly in the past few years, his beard fully grey and his eyes slightly cloudy. Deep crevasses cut lines through his forehead and around his mouth. Tobacco stains tinged the edge of his moustache a dirty yellow color. His face had always told a story of rough living with scars and a twisted nose but Miles spotted a few newer ones that shone pink.

"We've missed you." Nester looked to the whisky glass. "Looks like you missed us too."

"That couldn't be farther from the truth."

"You should put those fists to better use than using them to beat soft lads like that boy."

"My fists do not need a use."

Nester grinned, revealing chipped, yellow teeth and gaps. Miles struggled to understand why he had ever looked up to the man. His only reasoning was that the man was so far removed from his father who had such high expectations of Miles.

"You can pretend to be some hoity, toity lord all you like but some people just don't have it in their blood. You have fighting in you, my lad. Just look at you. Even in those posh clothes, you can't disguise it. You were meant for more exciting things than sitting in some large house in the middle of the countryside, listening to rich people complain and gossip."

Miles shook his head. “Sorry, Nester, I’ve put my fighting days behind me.”

He pursed his lips, making his moustache bristle. “We’ll see you back here soon enough when you realize what you really are.”

Ignoring him, Miles moved past and stepped outside. Jenkins had made himself scarce and for that, Miles was grateful. The last thing he needed to do tonight was prove Nester right—that under all the manners and clothes, he was no better than any of them.

Chapter Fifteen

AUGUSTA KEPT HER HANDS in her lap, watching the dancers swirl by. She crossed her eyes and uncrossed them but could find no joy in making everyone appear ludicrous. She wore her finest gown yet, a cream affair of silk overlaid with delicate lace. It had been cinched so tight she almost had breasts. Her hair had taken a good two hours to style. She almost missed the days when it was just pulled back tightly with a few curls around her face.

And what a waste of time all the preparation had been.

A minuet was announced and dancers hastened to get in line. All of Hampshire society and many more were here tonight. All here for the same reason—to celebrate her fiancé's return.

She twined her fingers tightly together and kept her back straight, urging her muscles to keep her upright and for her expression to remain neutrally content. It was all she could do to resist dropping at the waist and pressing her face into her hands.

"I cannot believe I am in this position again," she lamented to Joanna, who had remained steadfastly at her side all night. Chloe had also kept her company aside from the one dance with her fiancé.

Her gaze strayed to Miles. He had remained away from her and she suspected it was these rumors that was forcing him to keep his distance though she had not heard anything more about them. Whatever he had done to find the culprit, apparently he'd put a stop to the chatter.

He met her gaze and she regretted she'd even looked his way. He cut a fine figure as usual, even if he remained at the edges of the ballroom, watching the dancers with a dark intensity. Every fiber of her longed to rush to his side and take comfort in his arms and it made her muscles ache to remain where she was—the neglected fiancée once more.

"I cannot believe he has not arrived yet," Chloe muttered. "What is wrong with the man?"

Augusta gave a little shrug, feeling her chin wobble. There was fashionably late and there was this. Henry appeared to be showing no sign of attending. She frowned. He'd been so remorseful of what he had put her through, it was hard to fathom he would leave her here alone. No one had acknowledged his distinct absence to her but it was only a matter of time and she had little idea what she would say once it happened. What sort of a woman had no idea why her fiancé was not attending the ball thrown in his honor in his own house?

"Perhaps something has happened," mused Joanna. "You said he had seemed very apologetic and genuine?"

Augusta nodded. "I really believed he regretted how he had treated me."

"But to do it all over again." Chloe folded her arms. "I should give him a piece of my mind."

"I should give him more than that," said Joanna, "but perhaps we should find out the truth of the matter first. Why do you not speak to his brother? He must have some knowledge of Henry's whereabouts surely?"

Augusta shook her head vigorously. "I cannot."

"Why not?" Joanna gave her a look. "Has something else happened between you?"

Augusta wanted to lie but she never had been any good at falsehoods. She lifted a shoulder. "He came to speak with me prior to Henry's return. It was...well, it does not matter. He has made it clear he regrets his actions and with that gossip going around, I cannot possibly be seen to be sharing secrets with him."

"Well, no one can say anything of me." Joanna stood and cut a path through the throngs of people until she reached Miles's side. They both glanced her way then talked in earnest. She saw Joanna lift her hands in what appeared to be dismay.

Augusta swallowed. Perhaps Henry had decided he'd been foolish to return and had vanished again. If so, she could break things off without fear of reprise. Though it still did not help her future. She would most certainly become a penniless spinster then.

Joanna leaned in and Miles bowed his head to speak to her over the noise of the orchestra. She envied Joanna then, being so close to Miles. If only she could speak to him without fear, if only she could...well, none of it mattered anyway. He had only ever shown great remorse over any interactions with her. There was no sense on dwelling on what would never be.

Joanna returned to join them and drew out her fan to waft it rapidly in front of her face. "I loathe the heat of these places."

"You do look a little peaked," Augusta pointed out.

"Well?" demanded Chloe. "What excuse does he have for his brother's behavior?"

"No excuse. In fact, I think he is angrier at him than any of us." Joanna snapped the fan shut. "He said his brother was here this morning and he had to head out but vowed he would be home in time for the ball. Lord Ashwick has little idea where he went."

Augusta scowled. She never would expect Henry to lie to his brother. Despite Henry's recent behavior, he and Miles had a great respect for one another. She recalled many a time when Henry would speak of his brother in only the kindest of terms. What could be so urgent that he needed to leave and stay away from a ball thrown for him?

"I doubt he has gone forever," Joanna assured her.

Pursing her lips, Augusta blew out a breath. "Perhaps not. Either way, I feel foolish indeed for accepting him back into my life. Especially when I was making great progress in showing that I did not need him,"

"Well, you can still show him. There is no need for you to be a wallflower tonight." Joanna tugged on her dance card. "I have seen several men glance longingly at you. There would be no shame in dancing to pass the time."

"I suppose..."

"Oh, Mr. Henley, are you looking for a dance partner?" Joanna said to one of the gentlemen who had been stealing looks their way, though Augusta thought it was more in the direction of Joanna than her. "Miss Snow is looking to dance now. She was feeling a little delicate but do you not think a lively dance will help perk her up?"

"Oh, um." Mr. Henley tugged at his cravat. "Of course, Miss Snow, I should be delighted." He gave a little bow.

Augusta grimaced but took up the offer and allowed herself to be escorted out into the center of the ballroom for a quadrille. Mr. Henley was a fine dancer, though his fragrance was too strong and it made her wrinkle her nose to fight the desire to sneeze. However, Joanna's plan had worked and by the time she had finished, several men asked to fill out her dance card. Although her heart and feet felt heavy, at least it passed the time better than staring at the various entrances into the rooms, waiting for Henry to arrive. Not one gentleman asked her about Henry, either, much to her relief.

After three dances, she stepped back to retrieve a drink. "You did wonderfully," Joanna said, flipping open her fan and wafting it in Augusta's face.

Augusta closed her eyes and took pleasure in the brief respite from the growing heat of the room and her exertion. When she opened them and straightened, she released a small squeak as the back of her heel connected with something. She staggered backward a step to connect with a solid body. She did not need to turn to know who it was.

Breath held, she turned slowly and lifted her gaze upward. Even if she'd wanted to take another breath, she could not have. From a distance, Miles was handsome and beautiful, like a stone statue that one could admire in cold indifference. When he was up close, however, there was nothing cool about her. Even if she was not already warm from dancing, he would have set ablaze under her skin.

Every inch of him sparked of intensity, as though he were a thunderstorm threatening to shoot off lightning bolts. She had heard of a man once who had survived a lightning strike and he'd talked of how the hair on his head stood on end and his scalp prickled before he was hit. That was exactly how she felt right now.

"Miles," she said, cringing at her breathy tone.

"I was wondering if I might have the next dance."

She glanced around him, aware of a few gazes watching their interaction. "Are you certain we should?"

"If I cannot dance with who I want in my own house, then what's the point in even holding these infernal balls?"

"But you do not like dancing," she pointed out.

"I forgot that I should defer to Miss Snow before deciding what I do and do not like. Forgive me, I will not forget again."

"No, that is not what I meant...it is just..."

"You have danced with many men tonight, Gus. One dance with me will do no harm. In fact, I think it better that we dance rather than spend all evening avoiding each other, as though the gossips were correct."

She bit down on her bottom lip. "I suppose you are right."

"High praise indeed."

She rolled her eyes at him and allowed herself the first proper smile of the night. "A man like yourself does not need my praise, Miles."

"There you are wrong. Praise from a beautiful woman means more than praise from a single one of my contemporaries."

Warmth rose up in her face and she tried to will away the soft feeling his words created in her chest. To think she was so simple as to fall for a tiny compliment. Of course, it was not the compliment so much that had the effect but the source of it.

The next dance was announced, saving her from replying. They lined up for the slow country dance that most of the guests were pleased to partake in. It was an easier one for those who were not so sure footed or less inclined to dance the vigorous reels. It also gave the dancers plenty of time to talk. However, for the first few beats, Miles remained silent.

Augusta was not certain she trusted herself with anything so she remained quiet too, following the simple steps until they were in the center together, palm to palm. She swallowed hard and kept her focus ahead of her.

"I am sorry," he said finally.

"Whatever for?"

"Henry, of course."

"You do not need to apologize for him."

"Of course I do. He's my brother, my responsibility."

Augusta turned to look at Miles. "He is a grown man, what can you do? Lock him in a dungeon?"

"If I had one, I'd be damned tempted to." They split apart, ending up on opposite sides of the line. Augusta clapped her hands in time with the music until it was time for them to meet again, this time turning around one another.

"Do not blame yourself," she said.

"How can I not when you have spent half of the evening looking heartbroken?" He shook his head. "You would make a fine gothic heroine, Gus, and all men would wish to come to your aid and make you smile again."

"I had rather thought I was doing a fine job of looking utterly complacent."

"You were, I suppose. But I noticed." His gaze locked onto hers as they did one last twirl. "I always notice you, Gus."

Chapter Sixteen

GUESTS DEPARTED AND the crowds thinned, leaving a few stragglers determined to draw out the last of the entertainment as the grey light of dawn dripped in through the long windows of the ballroom. Miles was ready for the event to be over but he doubted he'd sleep. Damn his brother. How could he do this to Augusta? There was no sign of him still. After all the promises he'd made to her...

He finished the last dregs of his glass of port and put the glass down, too hard for the delicate crystal. The stem shattered and he winced at the sting that cut into his fingers. Shaking his head at himself, he put his finger to his mouth and sucked away the worst of the damage.

He scanned the room. A few people had mentioned Henry's absence and he had no doubt it fanned the flames of doubt surrounding Augusta and Henry's courtship. Dancing with her might not have been the best idea but seeing her looking so forlorn had torn a ragged hole in his heart. He couldn't resist a brief moment with her.

He scowled upon seeing Augusta's parents still lingering. Her friends had long since retreated home but there was no way they would still be here if Augusta had left the ball. So where the devil was she? It was easy to lose someone in the prior crowds but he'd known where she was for most of the night. He couldn't help himself. No matter how many times he tried to prevent his gaze from betraying him, it snuck over to her. She'd been exceptionally pretty tonight and he hated that it was all meant for Henry. His brother did not deserve her one jot.

Miles did a casual loop of the room, peering into some of the anterooms but there was no sign of her. He paused by the large windows, almost dismissing the thought that she would be outside until he caught sight of her by the lake. His scowl deepened. Augusta never set foot by that lake and he did not appreciate the sight of her there. It reminded him all too much of the day he'd nearly lost her.

Exiting the ballroom, he made haste to join her outside. Sunlight teased from behind the hills, bringing the promise of a bright and sunny day. A little mist from the damp grass rose and swirled about Augusta's skirts, making her look other-worldly. Her carefully styled hair had come free from its confines, leaving several curls dropping over her shoulders. She walked with her arms around her, her head bowed low, following the line of the lake.

"Gus!" he called.

She jerked her head up and stilled, a slight but tense smile flattening her lips. "Miles."

"What are you doing here?"

She pressed her lips together. "Walking, of course." she continued her slow pace around the generous, uneven edge of the water where reeds jutted up and concealed the threshold between water and land.

Miles mirrored her footsteps. "By the lake, though?"

She gave a light laugh. "Perhaps I was trying to be brave."

"I'd rather you did not."

"Do you think me foolish enough to fall in?" She wrapped her arms tighter about herself and peered ahead of her. "Well, I imagine many people think me a fool after tonight."

"Henry has a great deal of apologizing to do but no one thinks you a fool."

She twisted her head. "No? You cannot deny that I look silly indeed, waiting around for a fiancé for so long only for him to avoid me at his own ball."

"His behavior reflects only upon himself," he said through gritted teeth. He could wring his brother's neck for upsetting her.

"Do you think me a fool? For waiting so long?"

He shook his head. "Gus, you are one of the smartest women I know. A little too generous at times, but you are no fool."

"So I have been too generous to Henry," she murmured.

"Perhaps." Miles clamped his mouth shut before he said anything further. He'd love to tell her to end things with him but his motives were not pure enough for that sort of advice.

Augusta paused and sank onto the grass, plucking a reed and beginning to shred it in her fingers. Her white skirts spilled about her and she curled up her legs to one side, making her look like a delicate, creamy concoction. Miles hesitated. No one would think to look for either of them here and he'd already vowed he would not muddy the waters of their relationship again. But to see her so fragile, so small and in need of comfort—it would take a lot of willpower not to draw her into his arms and kiss away her pain.

Reluctantly, he sat next to her. “Henry will set a date,” he assured her. “I am not certain what he is going through at the moment but he was determined that he would marry you, Gus.”

He watched her expression, searching for some sign of delight or love or excitement at the idea. She did still love Henry, did she not?

She kept her gaze focused on the reed in her hand while she ripped at it, making it smaller and smaller. “Your father’s death had a great impact on Henry.”

“It did.”

“I wonder if your father had not died, whether he would have offered for my hand.”

“The two of you were always meant to be together. Everyone knew that.”

She glanced sideways at him and smiled. “You did not answer my question.”

“Questioning such things is not helpful.”

“Do you think we were always meant to be together, Miles?”

He clenched his jaw. It would be so easy to plant seeds of doubt, to ensure that she and Henry were never together again. But it would mean nothing. Henry was an ass for his current behavior but he had always been the better of them. If he could sort himself out, he’d be the best husband for Augusta, Miles was certain of that.

“You always seemed to like him,” he said vaguely.

“Yes, I suppose I did.” She looked down. “Oh, you’re bleeding!”

Frowning, he peered at his hand. A well of blood had pooled on his palm—enough to make it drip through his fingers. He grimaced. He'd completely forgotten he'd even cut himself. "Had a little fight with a glass." He tilted his lips. "The glass won."

"I can see that." Augusta retrieved a handkerchief from her bodice before he could fish out his own and forcefully grabbed his hand. Swiftly, she wrapped the delicate fabric around his large palm and pressed down upon it.

He swallowed at the sight of her delicate, pale fingers upon his slightly tanned and worn skin. Too much time fighting had left his knuckles scarred, tiny white strips crisscrossing over them. In the pale light of dawn, the marks seemed brighter.

He wished he could will them away—will his past away even. Go back to a time when his hands were scar-less and smooth. He could not help but wonder if he had never fallen down the hole of drinking, fighting, and gambling, would he have been able to court Augusta? Make her his? Or was it simply that she and Henry really were always meant to be together? After all, they were closer in age and Henry's temperament complimented Augusta's. Miles's quieter disposition was no use to her. Together, the two of them would be about the quietest couple in the *ton*.

His train of thought came to a standstill when he felt her soft fingers brush across his knuckles.

"I have ruined your glove."

She glanced at the discarded garment in question, the white fabric marred by a small red stain. "They are not my favorite."

"Well, that is a relief."

"How did you get so many scars?" she asked, continuing her torturous exploration of his hands with her own. Her thumb fell upon a particularly large scar that was still puckered.

"Fighting," he murmured reluctantly.

"And this one?"

"All fighting."

She tilted her head. "What sort of fights?"

"Gus..." he protested, voice tight.

"Was this when you went away?"

He shook his head. If he were a clever man, he'd stand up now and ignore her incessant questioning. Unfortunately for him, he had to be about the stupidest man in England.

He remained where he was, reveling in the feel of her soft fingertips, drawing in the sweet fragrance of her, and taking far too much pleasure in the way her dark lashes fanned out against slightly shimmering, pale skin as she studied his hands. Her distraction gave him far too much time to absorb the sight of her.

He most definitely was the stupidest man in England. Why the hell did he want to prolong his torture?

At least he would remember this...remember her. Once she was married and wrapped up in life with Henry, he could recall sitting here and feeling as though he was in the presence of the sweetest, prettiest woman he'd ever known. He smirked to himself. His warped humor and gruff ways were certainly no good for her. No wonder she had always been drawn to Henry.

"Why did you fight, Miles?"

He blew out a breath. Here he was hoping her curiosity would wane. Did he know nothing about women? It seemed so.

"Who can say? Sometimes because I had to. Sometimes because I wanted to."

There, that would scare her away.

"Why did you want to?"

Damn her.

"Because I was hungry for blood." He released a dry laugh. "And a fool."

She peered up at him, her eyes wide. "I think you are one of the cleverest men I have known."

"Then I think perhaps you are the fool, Gus."

Her lips curved slightly. "Did I not just say that I was?"

It would be so damn easy. There was no one around, no one to catch them. The last place anyone would expect Augusta to be would be by the lake so her parents certainly would not come searching for her. He even suspected he could have her eager and willing for him.

But that was only because of Henry's foolish neglect of her.

Christ, his brother did not even know what he had here. Augusta kissed with the passion of a thousand women. She was open and eager and a quick learner. All he would have to do is lean in and brush his lips over hers. She'd taste of wine maybe or even brandy snaps. If he pressed her down against the grass, he'd be able to explore her body with his hands, take in the feel of her lithe body in a way that he'd never been allowed to do. He'd commit it all to memory and relive the moment forever.

Swallowing hard, he removed her hand from his and eyed the dry cut. "Another scar to add to my collection." He handed her back her handkerchief. "And it seems I owe you gloves and a handkerchief."

"That handkerchief was my favorite," she said with a smile.

He narrowed his gaze at her. "Are you teasing me, Gus?"

"A little. Does it feel strange?"

"No." He shook his head. "No, I quite like it."

"Miles, I—" She pressed a palm to his chest and his heart came to a standstill. Her lips parted, her eyes darkened, pupils wide. He heard her intake of breath. This was it, the moment he could steal for himself. Every fiber of his being warred against each other, making him feel as though he were being torn in two. He wanted to kiss her more than anything in the world but there was no forgetting that she was Henry's bride-to-be.

Whatever mistakes he'd made while Henry was away, whatever idiocy his brother was involved in to make him behave this way, Miles could not betray him. Not again.

"Your parents are likely looking for you," he said hastily. "We had better return to the ballroom."

"Oh."

He could think of a few harsher ways to put it. Drawing up his shoulders, he stood and offered her a hand. She took it and allowed him to aid her to her feet. As soon as she was stable, he withdrew his hand. "The day looks to be growing pleasant. I think I may take a walk."

"Oh," she said again.

"Are you broken, Gus?"

She shook her head vigorously and gave a bright smile. "No, of course not, though I am a little tired."

"I would escort you in but I suspect you and I arriving together after vanishing would not be the cleverest of ideas."

"No, of course. You are right."

“Stay away from the lake edge,” he warned as he turned away. “I have little desire to take a dip today.” He didn’t look back but he could have sworn he heard her mutter about what an ass he was. Blast, the woman just could not help making him smile.

Chapter Seventeen

"I REALLY THINK I SHOULD speak with your father." Augusta's mother wrung her hands together, pacing the length of the oriental rug in the drawing room before turning and repeating the movement.

Augusta resisted pinching the bridge of her nose and lowered herself onto the sofa to retrieve her embroidery. She peered at her unfinished pattern without really seeing it. All she could remember was yesterday.

Yes, the embarrassment warmed her cheeks, yes she was mightily frustrated at Henry and it made her feel hot and prickly.

However, most of that warmth came from having sat with Miles at the end of the ball.

She could have sworn he was going to kiss her. She frowned. Or perhaps she was wrong. If only she understood men a little better, though she had a suspicion one could know everything about the world of men and still find Miles a conundrum. If he really was going to kiss her, did that mean the others were not really a mistake? Did he harbor some feelings for her or was it simply fanciful thinking? Goodness, how many times could someone repeat the same mistake?

"We have been patient enough with Henry," her mother continued. "I think it is time your father spoke with Miles again."

"No!" Augusta bit down on her lip as her mother's eyes widened at the veracity of the comment.

"We must do what is best, Gus Gus." Her mother shook her head and sank onto the sofa next to her, flattening the cushions so that Augusta ended up leaning into her mother's ready embrace without leaving her a choice.

"I just think...that Miles is trying his best. I do not believe it will benefit us to berate him for his brother's behavior."

Her mother swiftly disentangled herself from Augusta and stood, pacing again. "You are right. The last thing we should wish to do is aggravate the man. After all, he is the man in charge of funding his brother. The last thing we wish to do is encourage him to cut your future husband off."

"Mother! That is cold."

She sighed and gave Augusta a look. "I have tried not to be, believe me." She gave a soft smile. "We were so happy when Henry proposed. You are so good together and he really is the most affable of men. We knew he'd treat you well and he has the finances to ensure you are looked after when we are gone."

"Oh, Mama..."

"I try not to put this on you but you are clever and I know you are not ignorant to the ways of the world."

Augusta nodded. How could a woman ever forget her standing in this world? She had known since she was a young girl—her main duty was to marry and marry well. It was easy for those who were fair and lovely with bright personalities that ensured they garnered attention from more than one suitor. For her, she had always known that once Henry had proposed, that was it—her one chance.

"If Henry continues this behavior..."

Augusta set down her embroidery to the side of her. "Mama, I am certain there was good reason for his lack of attendance," she assured her. "He was most sincere in his apology to me upon his return. Do not fret."

Her mother's shoulders lost their stiff appearance. "I suppose you are right. There must have been good reason and Henry was never the sort to betray his promises."

"Precisely," she said with more confidence than she felt. However, it would not do for her parents to fret over her future nor would it help for them to get involved. Especially when she was feeling as confused as she was. How did one let go of a path that one had been set on for so long? How did one explain that it was for no other reason than that she was developing feelings for a man who might not even want her?

Oh Lord, who was she kidding? Her feelings were not developed. They were fully flourished, seeping into every inch of her and overtaking her until she could not see sense.

"I think I might go for a walk," Augusta said, standing so quickly that it made her head swirl a little and she had to pause.

Her mother blinked at her. "A walk?"

"Yes, I could do with the fresh air. I am still a little fatigued after the ball."

"You do look a little wan."

"See? Some air will do me well."

Augusta retrieved her bonnet and a light spencer jacket with ruched shoulders. She escaped quickly, tying her bonnet as she went and drawing in breaths of fresh summer air. Wildflowers lined the edge of the dirt road away from her house, specks of white and purple interlaced with the occasional yellow. She plucked up a purple one, carrying it with her as though it was keeping her company on her walk.

Though she walked briskly, making her limbs feel warm and her heart pound quickly, none of it could erase the deep, uncertain feeling that lingered in the depths of her stomach. It bunched there, occasionally fluttering up to her chest and throat, making it feel tight.

She knew what she needed to do but she was not certain she had the courage. If only she were more like Joanna or Chloe...or almost anyone. How she wished she was anyone but her.

"Augusta."

She stilled at the sound of her name being called, her heart giving a flutter for the briefest of moments until she realized Miles rarely called her Augusta and Henry's tones were not as deep. She twisted on her heel to find him striding toward her. She smiled softly. He did look handsome in his buckskins and cravat. Most women would envy her indeed being alone with him, let alone being engaged to him.

"I owe you an apology."

Yes, you do, she wanted to say but the words dissolved on her tongue. For all her talk of being bolder and trying to learn to flirt better and show him she was not just some shy, quiet wallflower who had sat around waiting for him, she had not changed one jot.

"Oh, no..." she began.

Henry held up a hand. "I know I do." He gestured in the direction of her house. "I was coming to apologize to you and your parents when I saw you walking. I will still accompany you to your house if you do not mind."

She exhaled slowly. Really, she wanted more time to walk alone. Being in Henry's company was confusing. He was so pleasant and handsome and everything a woman should want. She found it hard to think for herself with him around. It seemed every time she had a singular thought, he blew it away like a cloud of smoke with his charming and reasonable words. "Of course," she finally said, letting her shoulders drop.

"I had somewhat of an emergency the other night," he explained as they began their stroll back toward the house.

"I see."

"If I could have been there, I would have, I promise you." He tugged at his cravat, making Augusta scowl. She could not say she knew him as well as she had always thought but that simple movement was an odd one. If there was anything Henry was not, it was disconcerted.

"Everyone was there to see you," she said. "You were certainly missed."

And she looked like a fool. She bunched her hands. And she was angry. So, so angry. Really, he deserved a lashing with her tongue.

"I know. You must forgive me, Augusta."

"What was the emergency?"

"It was of an, ugh, sensitive matter."

"Sensitive matter?"

"But I am here to make amends you see." He smiled warmly.

"I see."

"You are angry at me?"

She sighed. Of course she was. What woman would not be? But the words would not come. The lashing she ought to give rose up briefly then vanished under a haze of cowardice. "I thank you for apologizing."

"It will not happen again," he vowed.

"We shall have to organize something else. Much of society wished to see you."

"Of course. Perhaps a dinner at Charlecote shall do the trick."

"Perhaps," she murmured, aware her stomach did a somersault at the thought of being across the table from Miles.

"Are your parents angry at me?"

"My mother is a little disconcerted perhaps. She could not understand why you would not be there," she said, "but I suspect my father did not notice."

"I shall grovel at her feet if I must."

"I rather think she would be entirely embarrassed if you did such a thing."

Henry grinned. "Would you rather I groveled at yours?"

"Certainly not!"

"If it is of any comfort to you, I have already had my ears practically boxed by Miles."

"Henry, you do not need to apologize further." Especially if it meant him speaking of his brother. His apologies sounded sincere and even if she could not fathom what sort of sensitive matter would keep him away all night or why he could not tell her of it, she would really rather forget the whole matter. It had been too embarrassing and horrible and disconcerting.

"You really are a wonderful girl," Henry said. "I'm lucky no one decided to snap you up whilst I was gone."

Augusta ignored the slightly patronizing tone and concentrated on keeping her expression neutral. The last thing he needed to know about was her and Miles and their silly kisses. The brothers had always been close and she would never wish to be responsible for ruining their relationship over what had to be just a big mistake.

Well, two big mistakes.

Nearly three.

"Henry," she began but any thoughts of trying to talk openly with him fled when she spotted a gentleman walking along the country path that met the road just ahead. Although, *gentleman* was a bit of a stretch. She had not seen Mr. Jenkins since the day Miles had punched him and for that she was grateful. What was he doing here, near her house, she did not know, and nor did she wish to.

"Perhaps we should just walk..."

Mr. Jenkins waved a hand in greeting. "Miss Snow."

Her stomach sank. Henry would be nothing but polite and she could not think of a reason to ignore him without explaining about the rumors and her silly attempt at trying to get Henry home. Henry introduced himself to Mr. Jenkins and the men briefly conversed but Augusta could feel Mr. Jenkins's gaze upon her. The flicker behind his eyes felt predatory, as though she were some delicate prey that he wished to put between his teeth and snap the neck of.

She cast her gaze behind him, focusing on the ancient oak tree that had been there for likely hundreds of years. How she envied that tree with its strong roots and firm trunk. She felt more like a seed, blowing on the wind, her future being dictated by the breath of others. If she had half the strength of that tree, she would stomp her feet, declare that Mr. Jenkins was a scoundrel and that she was indeed still angry with Henry.

But, no. She had none of it. Instead she forced a polite smile and listened to them discuss her and her marriage to Henry, all the while suffering under Mr. Jenkins's predatory stare.

She finally loosened a breath when Mr. Jenkins bid them farewell and she and Henry continued their walk back to the house.

"Seems a decent chap that Jenkins."

"I do not like him one jot," she muttered.

"Pardon?"

Augusta bit down on her bottom lip. "Oh, nothing."

Lord, if only she were not such a coward.

Chapter Eighteen

MILES GLANCED AT THE drinks cabinet in the library. He only kept the damned thing around because the piece of furniture was over one hundred years old and purchased by his grandfather. Now, he was wishing he'd rid himself of the thing as soon as he had inherited his title. Dark, carved mahogany inlaid with ivory and jade tempted him with what lay behind it—whisky, brandy, and several other liquors—kept for visitors and guests—but tempting nonetheless.

He shook his head to himself. He was losing his wits. Drink rarely tempted him these days and he could indulge the odd one with no problems. However, tonight he just knew if he pulled the cork on one of those bottles, he would drink himself into a stupor—something he had not done in many years.

With one last glance at the cabinet, he rose from the desk, his chair screeching upon wooden floors. He rubbed a hand across his face and doused the lamps, retrieving a candle to carry through the darkened corridors with him until he reached the main drawing room. From there he could observe the front entrance to the house and watch out for Henry. He shook his head as he stepped into the drawing room and lit several candles from his own, glancing at the clock. His mother had long retreated to bed, unconcerned by Henry's lack of presence at dinner. He had lots of friends to visit and one could not expect him to wish to spend every hour with his family, she had said.

Miles pressed his lips together and sank onto the sofa. Henry was indeed popular and no doubt had many friends to catch up with but what their mother did not know, was that many were commenting on the fact that they had barely seen Henry since his return. The fact was, his brother was acting strange indeed. Just yesterday, he had rose early and spent the morning goodness knows where. Given none of his acquaintances were prone to early mornings, Miles could not fathom it.

Suppressing a yawn, he set the candle to one side. If only he'd have thought to have a pot of coffee but all the servants were in bed and he was not inclined to wake them. Anyway, despite the fact his eyes were heavy and gritty, he would not sleep—not until Henry had returned and told him what the devil was going on. None of this behavior was becoming of a man about to be married and, by God, if Henry was involved in something untoward...

No, surely not? Henry had always been the good brother. Running off and travelling the world might not be considered the most gentlemanly behavior in a fiancé, but it was nowhere near as torrid as what Miles had ended up involved in. Whatever was going on, he could not bring himself to believe that Henry had been so foolish as to follow in his older brother's footsteps.

He jerked awake at the sound of a door shutting, his chin slipping from where it had been propped on his hand. He blinked in the dim light and took a moment to orientate himself. Gone were the images of Augusta that had floated temptingly behind his eyelids. Instead, his brother stepped into the room, scowling when he saw Miles.

"What the devil are you still doing up?" Henry asked.

Miles glanced over his brother, noting his incorrectly tied cravat and ruffled hair. "I could ask you the same."

Henry lifted a shoulder. "Oh, just visiting with friends."

Miles rose to his feet and rubbed the knot that was gathering at the back of his neck. "Were you drinking?"

"Barely. Now, if you do not mind, I am hideously tired. I should—"

Miles stepped in front of his brother before he could leave the drawing room.

"This is not the first time you have returned home in the early hours."

Henry lifted a brow. "I did not know you were my keeper, Miles."

"Funnily enough, I am. In case you have forgotten, once I inherited the title, that is almost exactly what I became."

Henry laughed then frowned. "Good God, you are not jesting."

"I have made excuse after excuse for your absence and let you be for too long in the hopes you would return on your own. Now that you are home, you are hardly here and you have been neglecting your fiancée most terribly." Miles blew out a breath. "Goddamn it, Henry, you should have seen her at the ball..."

His brother's expression turned sheepish. "I know, Miles, really I do, and I apologized most heartily to her and we shall set a date very soon. You need not worry. I shall do my duty."

"Your duty started as soon as you proposed to her," he said between clenched teeth. Damn, if he was her fiancé, he'd never let her out of his sight. He'd have her wed in a heartbeat and certainly not out at all hours and neglecting to dance with her and make her the happiest woman on earth.

Henry glanced him over. "You have changed a lot, Miles. Since when did you begrudge a man a little time before wedding and settling down?"

"Since you showed that you cannot be trusted," Miles bit out. "Where have you even been? What is so important that you would continue to neglect your fiancée?" Miles narrowed his gaze at him. "Are you drinking? Gambling? fighting?"

Henry snorted. "I'm not you, Miles."

He took a step back, shaking his head. His brother was not wrong—Henry had never been like him and despite his odd behavior, he would never do the things that he did. It did not mean the jab did not strike true, however. He shoved a hand through his hair. "It has been a long time since I have done any of those things."

Henry nodded. "And do you really think, having seen what you went through, that I would do the same?"

"Yet you can still offer me no explanation for your whereabouts?"

"What is this? The Spanish inquisition?" Henry went to move past him. "I'm exhausted and I have a need to find my bed."

Miles stepped to the side, blocking his exit. "I know when you are lying to me, Henry. If you are in trouble..."

"I am in no trouble, Brother. If you believe nothing else, then believe that." Henry's shoulders sagged. "Do not fear, I shall do the right thing, just as I promised."

Miles searched his brother's sincere gaze before relenting and stepping back. "If you let Augusta down again..."

"I can expect a beating?" Henry's lips quirked.

"You know I am excellent at delivering them."

"Too much practice in your past."

Miles closed his eyes briefly. He would never win a fight with his brother when Henry had ended up being far too involved in Miles's sordid history. "Just cease being a cad. You have not seen the hurt you caused Gus. It is not pleasant to behold, believe me."

"Gus?"

"You know full well that's been her nickname since childhood," he said irritably.

"I do but I did not know you used it."

Miles glared at his brother. "Does it matter what I call her? Concern yourself with actually spending time with your fiancée."

"I told you, Miles, I have every intention of doing right by her. I just need to...see to some things."

Miles folded his arms across his chest. "What things? Surely you have had enough damned years to put things in order."

Henry made a frustrated noise. "Last time I looked, you are not our mother. Now, cease making yourself gray and flapping like an old woman." Henry turned on his heel and strode across the room, pulling open a drawer in the writing desk that faced the south window. Withdrawing a bottle of liquor, he grinned. "I am awake now thanks to you so I shall be taking this to bed."

Grinding his teeth together, Miles stepped aside. Apparently Henry would not listen to sense and he doubted he'd figure out what he was up to by mere discussion.

"Oh by the by, you did not, perchance, assign someone to follow me, did you?"

Miles scowled. That had been his next thought but as much as he wanted to know what the hell his brother was up to, he was not certain he would go as far as to stoop to such methods. "You really think I have the time to do such a thing?"

His brother shrugged. "I had a distinct impression I was being followed tonight."

"Perhaps it was because you were in places you should not be?"

"God's teeth, Miles, I was in a perfectly respectable area and I have little desire to report back to you about my every move."

"We've never lied to one another, Henry."

A flash of guilt crossed his face before being hidden behind a raised chin. "Simply because I do not wish to detail my whereabouts at all times does not mean I'm lying to you."

"Does it not?"

"Anyway, I saw this chap several times. Gray-haired, scruffy looking. I think he had a scar." Henry motioned down the side of his face.

Miles wrapped a hand into a fist. It couldn't be, could it? Why would Nester be following Henry? God damn that Jenkins. He would never have set foot in the Bell Inn if the idiot had not been behaving so terribly. Miles tossed aside the thought. It had been years since he'd worked with Nester. There had been nothing stopping him from approaching Miles so why would he show a sudden interest in his brother?

"Sounds as though you are being paranoid," Miles said as lightly as he could.

"With a brother like you hovering over me like a mama at Almack's, can you blame me?"

"If you were not sneaking around, you would have no need for blame."

"Bloody hell, Miles, I was not sneaking. I was simply..." He shook his head. "It's too hard to explain and I can see well enough where your loyalties lie."

Miles let his frown deepen. "What is that meant to mean?"

Henry laughed. "Is it not obvious? You would rather watch out for your beloved Gus than your own brother. Hell, if you care that much about her, perhaps you should marry her." He snatched a glass from the side and hugged the bottle of liquor close. "Now, if you will excuse me, I am bone-tired and hankering for my bed. Perhaps you could be so kind as to tell your lackeys to leave me alone."

"I have no lackeys," Miles replied tightly.

"Whatever you say." Still clasping the glass, Henry gave him a clumsy salute and paced out of the room.

Miles finally unfurled his fists and strode over to the windows to stare out over the gardens. He squinted into the darkness as though he might be able to see some movement or a flash of gray hair. After many moments of nothing, he moved away from the window. Why would Nester be interested in him after all this time? Henry was most certainly being paranoid, and if his brother was feeling such things, it had to mean he was doing something untoward, surely?

And why the devil did Henry have to say that about him and Gus? Now, he wouldn't have a moment's rest because all he would be thinking of was how much he wanted just that—to marry Gus and have her all to himself. He rubbed a hand over his face and smothered a yawn. What a royal mess this all was.

Chapter Nineteen

"AT LEAST YOUR TROUSSEAU is ready," her mother murmured.

Augusta nodded vaguely, keeping her attention fixed on the book in her hands.

"Now that Henry has set a date, we have an awful lot to do."

Augusta nodded again and raised the book higher in front of her face to hide her grimace. Henry had indeed set a date and appeared to be sticking to his promise of being more reliable. That did not, however, stop the sinking feeling in her stomach that she was about to embark on the biggest mistake of her life.

"What a beautiful bride you shall make," her mother enthused from her position at the drawing table. Stacks of paper were laid out in front of her, and Augusta did not need to steal a look to know that Mama was writing to just about the whole country to let them know a date had been set. She grimaced again and forced her attention onto the words in front of her. Unfortunately, her attention would not commit itself and the letters seemed to jumble in front of her eyes.

"Naturally—"

Standing abruptly, Augusta dropped the book on the side table with a thud. Her mother blinked at her. "Gus?"

"Forgive me, Mama, I appear to have a sudden headache. I think I shall retreat to my room for a while."

"Oh, of course, you go rest." She waved a hand. "These preparations can be so taxing on a young woman."

She gave her mother a weak smile and hastened out of the room and upstairs, lifting her skirts so she could take them two at a time. She tugged open the door and shut it swiftly behind her, staring at it for a moment as though someone might follow her. Not that anyone would.

A rustle and the creak of a window made her spin on her heel. "You..." The word came out a startled, harsh whisper. She staggered a couple of steps in retreat until her back met the wood of the door.

Mr. Jenkins turned from the slightly open window, a sheepish smile on his face. "I thought you would be in the drawing room for a little longer."

The confused haze cleared swiftly. Her heart slammed hard in her chest, sending her pulse fluttering through her limbs and making them feel like liquid. "You...you were watching me..."

His smile curved and the heat in her body turned to pure ice. He took several steps toward her and she fumbled for the doorknob but her hands shook. She should scream but everything seemed to remain trapped in her throat, tangled in a web of horror. What was he doing here? In her room? How long had he been watching her?

"You are very intriguing." He moved closer and she ducked past him as a squeak of fear escaped her throat. She ended up by the fireplace, backed up against the decorative wood surround.

As he neared, she pressed herself into it, the hard edge of the wood digging deep into her back. She felt no pain from it.

Out of the periphery of her vision, she spotted the fireplace tools. She stretched her fingers but they were too far away now that he had edged closer.

"I think you should leave," she said in a dry whisper.

"I can get many women, you know."

"I'm sure you can."

"But you...you flourish all of a sudden then have the gall to turn me down." He shook his head with a chuckle. "I cannot help but find you fascinating."

"I am terribly dull, I assure you."

He flicked a speck of dust from his sleeve. "You have two brothers who find you just as intriguing as I do. I think you are wrong, dear Miss Snow."

She opened her mouth to refute that fact but it seemed pointless. For some reason, Mr. Jenkins had recognized from early on her feelings for Miles.

"If you leave now, I shall not tell anyone you were here."

"Or I could stay and teach you what to expect from your husband."

Her heart jammed up in her throat again, sending a fresh flood of panic through her. "Leave. Please," she begged softly.

He continued to come close and she glanced at the iron poker, standing a few feet from her. If she could just make her useless body move... But he was upon her, pressing his body into hers. He ran a finger down her face then fingered a curl not far from her collarbone. Bile burned at the back of her throat.

When she glanced into his eyes, there was no madness like she expected but a sort of cool, calmness. Mr. Jenkins thought that she owed him this, she could see that now. Her foolish flirtations had reached a man so entitled, that he thought she was his due.

Good Lord, what a silly fool she had been.

His warm breath whispered across her face and she could smell his expensive fragrance. She gulped hard and closed her eyes to his study of her. Even behind the comforting darkness of her lids, she felt his gaze travel across her, taking in every inch of her body and features. Her limbs ached something fierce from being so stiff but still they would not move. If she tried, she suspected she could shove him away long enough to either make a run for the door or snatch up that poker as a weapon.

Yet again, she was so terrified of life that she could do nothing but wait.

Warmth from his skin skimmed her face and she scrunched her eyes more tightly closed. Maybe he would realize she did not want this. Maybe he would see her fear and just leave. Maybe...

"I have had to ask myself what it is about you that has me so enraptured," he murmured. "But you really are quite beautiful." He laughed. "The only man who saw it was that idiot Ashwick and I regret I did not notice it sooner. If he had not been around, plaguing us with his looming presence, we could have spent time together sooner."

Plaguing her? Miles had not been plaguing her. Quite the opposite. He'd been protecting her and comforting her and trying to help her make the right decisions. Well, she would be damned if she let him down now.

"Leave," she said, opening her eyes and summoning enough courage to make the word hiss out of her.

"My dear Miss Snow..."

"Leave, I said." She put palms to his chest, registering how her hands trembled against the planes of his body. He was nowhere near as strong or tall as Miles but her fingers looked tiny and fragile against the breadth of him. Regardless, she lifted her gaze to his. "Whatever you think I did, you are wrong. A mere conversation does not preclude an affair and it certainly does not make you entitled to my body."

"I think—"

"I do not care what you think!" She gave him a shove. It was ineffectual but she had hardly used all her strength. Drawing in a breath, she summoned more, tightening her arms in case she needed to push him again.

"Are you really going to deny that you were not awfully bored of waiting for your fiancé? That you were looking for a little entertainment?"

"I was bored, certainly. I was, however, not looking for anything like this and I highly doubt any woman is."

Mr. Jenkin's skin began to grow red, a flush creeping up his neck and into his cheeks. She could hear the grinding of teeth. Nausea rolled in her stomach and she fought back the bitterness rising in her throat. He curled a hand deliberately slowly around one arm, then another. She flinched under his touch but he pinched hard, keeping her pinned.

"You cannot tease a man, Miss Snow. I think that is a lesson you should learn now."

His mouth lowered to hers.

No! It could not happen. The only man she had ever kissed had been Miles and that was how she wanted it to stay!

Shoving both palms against his chest with as much force as she could muster, she managed to create enough space between them for her to swing her knee straight up into his groin. A groan emitted from him and his eyes seemed to almost cross as he doubled over, his hands between his legs. She used the opportunity to grab the poker and brandish it in front of her as he staggered back a few steps.

"Know this, Mr. Jenkins," her voice trembled but she drew up her shoulders and forced her legs to remain firm, despite the urge to flee the room entirely, "should you come near me again, I shall happily stab you with a hat pin."

"Damn you," he hissed.

"I suggest you do as I originally asked and leave." She gestured toward the window with the poker.

He groaned and glanced at the open window. "You cannot expect me to..."

"You climbed in here and I assumed you had planned to climb out. You can manage."

"Not with bloody broken bollocks I cannot!"

"If they really are broken, I have done the whole of womankind a favor. You, sir, need to spend less time thinking with them." She gestured again to the window. "Leave or I shall have my father come up here with his shotgun. The rest of the world might not believe you broke in here but my father would take my word and happily shoot you."

His jaw ticked while he remained bunched over. For the first time, she heard how heavy her breaths were. She kept the poker stiff and steady, refusing to break eye contact. Finally, he turned to leave. As soon as his fingers were clear of the window, she slammed it shut. She almost hoped he fell if it were not for how horrified her parents would be should they find him in a crumpled heap beneath her window. Her parents would believe she had not invited him in, she was certain of that, but it would not take the housekeeper long to spread word of his visit.

She peered out of the window and watched him scurry away. The gall of the man! To believe that her politeness meant to invite him into her bedroom for a...a liaison! She never realized wearing new dresses and a touch of makeup would invite such behavior. But at least now, she knew the truth. Whoever she had pretended to be, it was not her. She did not enjoy the attention or the gossip it brought.

Slowly, she lowered the poker back to its holder and unfurled her fingers, eyeing the red marks from where she had held it so tightly.

A bubble of laughter escaped her as she recalled Mr. Jenkins's expression when her knee connected with his groin. He had not been expecting that from her! And, if she was honest, she had not been expecting it from herself.

Well, with any luck, he would never come near her again. She suspected he would go find a more willing woman and lose interest in her now. Augusta lowered herself onto the wide windowsill and pressed her heated forehead against the cool glass. She had lost sight of Mr. Jenkins fleeing from the house but he was likely over in the fields by now at the pace he was moving. She cast her gaze about the gardens and nodded to herself. Just wait until she told Joanna and Chloe what she had done—they would be so surprised.

And hopefully proud. She could not help feel proud of herself. She had finally stood up to a man and refused to let him dictate her moves. Now if only she could do that with the rest of her life...

A flicker in the sky from the corner of her eye caught her attention and she squinted at it. Smoke rose into the air, black and growing in thickness. She did not think the gardener had anything to burn and she had seen no bonfire prepared in the last few days. He usually did that in autumn after scraping up all the leaves.

The smoke grew darker, winding and billowing like an ominous storm cloud. She moved off the windowsill and pulled open the window once more. The acrid scent struck her immediately and she leaned out of the window to try to see the source of it.

Her heart jammed to a halt.

The stables.

Someone had set fire to the stables.

Augusta raced out of her bedroom and downstairs. "Fire," she yelled as she barreled outside in her delicate slippers, not waiting to find out if anyone had heard her as she sprinted to the stable block. There was no chance she was going to let her horses die.

Chapter Twenty

AS SOON AS HE'D ARRIVED at The Queen's Head inn, Miles recognized his mistake. He paused at the door and glanced back at his horse, now under the care of one of the grooms. This was what Nester wanted. Hell, he was pretty certain it was what a lot of people expected. Just a few years of playing viscount and Miles Stanton was ready to tumble back into his old life of drinking and gambling. He'd thought he was being clever going to one he'd never set foot in—as though that might save him from guilt. After all, he was not directly slipping back into his life if he was drinking at a new pub.

He muttered a curse to himself and stepped away from the front door, crushing down the ache in his gut that he so badly wanted to quash under the weight of reckless drinking and gaming. He had to continue to do better—no matter what. Even if Augusta was going to marry his brother, he still could not handle disappointing her, and as much as he told himself he'd only do it once, he knew how unlikely that was.

With more determined strides, he retrieved his horse and set off back home. He would bury himself in estate work rather than alcohol. He'd even damn well help Henry with wedding arrangements if he had to. It would be near agonizing but it was better than letting himself sink into the mire.

He rode swiftly, making quick work of the country roads that led back to town. From there, he cut across the fields that skimmed past the Waverly estate and Augusta's modest family home, reveling in the burn in his legs and arms while he drew in heavy breaths. He could have taken the country lane home but he needed the open expanses.

And a small, foolish part of him needed to see Augusta's home.

Miles grimaced to himself. No matter how hard he rode, no matter how much he worked, he was beginning to suspect he could never run or hide from his feelings for her. He would just have to resign himself to a lifetime of suffering. However, if she was happy with Henry, he would manage it.

On the rise of a gentle slope, he paused. The scent of smoke drifted across the fields and he scanned the expanse of countryside, his gaze landing upon billows of grey smoke. The jolt to his chest was immediate. It came from the direction of Augusta's house. Maybe it was deliberate—someone burning some shrubbery perhaps—however, it was rare to see a bonfire give up such thick smoke. He glanced down at the reins bunched in his gloved hands, already aware of what his decision was. He needed to go and find out—with haste.

"Sorry, girl, but you need to give it your all," he murmured to the horse, giving her a brief pat.

He rode with urgency, telling himself that it would be something innocent. Nothing dangerous. Nothing that could harm Augusta. But every inch of his being felt as though it were on alert. The hairs on the back of his neck were sticking on end, his breath was tight and not just from exertion. He just knew, down in his bones, he needed to get to her.

The closer he got, the more painful the tightness in his chest became. The smoke grew thicker and the stench covered the land. Flickers of flame grew visible, arching high into the air like the breath of an angry dragon. This was nothing innocent.

He tethered his horse on the gate at the garden to keep her away from the fire then sprinted the rest of the distance into the small cobbled courtyard. The modest-sized barn was fully ablaze. He could hardly see the roof now and orange flames licked out of the few windows. A groom ran back and forth with water buckets while Mrs. Snow stood in the doorway of the house, clasping a handkerchief in one hand.

"Oh, Miles..." She flung her arms around him as he arrived.

"Mr. Snow is in there," she sobbed against his neck. "He went to get Augusta but..."

"Gus?" He pulled back to eye Mrs. Snow's tear-streaked face.

"She was the first to spot the fire. She went in to get the horses."

Miles disentangled himself from her embrace and raced over to the blaze. Heat from the fire prickled his skin. "Keep trying to douse it," he ordered the exhausted-looking stable hand. He spotted two horses loose and clever enough to put plenty of distance between themselves and the fire. The Snows owned three, he knew that much, which explained why Augusta was still in the inferno.

Tearing off his jacket, he dunked it in the nearby water trough and put it back on, shuddering as droplets of frigid water trickled down his arms and neck. He undid his cravat and wrapped it around his mouth. Just as he was about to enter, someone emerged from the smoke. Bent double, Mr. Snow gagged and coughed, clawing his hands up Miles's chest, though Miles suspected he had little idea who he was. His face was black and his hair singed.

"Gus..."

Miles nodded and passed the man over to Mrs. Snow. "Get him some water," Miles ordered before ducking into the inferno.

The lack of windows did not help with visibility. No wonder Mr. Snow had been unable to find Augusta. Smoke filled the air, making his eyes water. He remained low and called her name, moving slowly in case she was on the ground. Smoke tickled the back of his throat and he fought the urge to cough while heat from above waved down, making him sweat. Flecks of flaming wood were beginning to drop down from the roof. He glanced up to see fire rippling along the beams, the only light in the gloom. It was a matter of time before the whole roof collapsed.

A desperate whinny from deep within the barn snared his attention. He squinted into the gloom, eyes burning. The sweat dripping into his eyes didn't help matters. But he had to get to Augusta.

He pushed on toward the back, cursing when his toe struck something hard and pain burst through his foot. Gritting his teeth, he continued moving through the smoke. The heat increased and the flames above were clouded by it, creating an eerie red glow. All around him wood popped and hissed and somewhere behind him, something cracked. He didn't take the time to look at what it was.

His palms finally came into contact with the body of the distressed horse. "Gus?" he called, the word muffled by the cravat around his mouth.

He dropped low and swiped the smoke and sweat from his eyes, all too aware he had no time for this. Much longer and the building would be down upon them. He scrabbled his hands across the ground until he came upon fabric. He bunched it in his hands and gave it a tug. It was most certainly attached to a body. He felt his way over to her and drew her limp form into his arms. As light as a feather and just as easy to handle, he slung her over his shoulder and grabbed the horse by its mane.

"Come on," he urged, tugging it forward.

With much persuasion, the terrified animal moved at a slow pace toward the entrance. A thin shaft of light broke through the choking thickness. The building was small but he felt as though he might as well be wading through an ocean to escape. His lungs were thick with smoke and his head swirled but the slender legs currently tucked under his arm and the limp arms tapping on his back as he moved urged him onward.

As they neared the front of the barn, the horse propelled itself forward, tearing from his grip and vanishing out of the entrance. Behind him, a crack reverberated through the air. He shifted Augusta fully into his arms and kept himself bent low, shielding her with his body and bracing himself for the moment that flaming wood and clay tiles collapsed atop him.

The pain never came and he continued forward as fast as his sluggish legs could carry him until they were out into daylight. He squinted in the light and gagged on a gulp of fresh air. Augusta was swiftly taken from him before he had even had a chance to check on her condition. The stable hand gaped up at the burning building while Miles sank onto the edge of the water trough. He took a scoopful of it and swiped it over his face before sipping the bitter water from his cupped hands. "It's lost, boy," he rasped to the stable hand.

"The horses are well, though." The lad nodded toward the three horses, now corralled into one of the fields. Even the one Miles had rescued appeared well.

Miles glanced wearily at the house, looking up to where he knew Augusta's room was. He only hoped he had reached her soon enough.

He watched as the barn began to collapse in on itself with an odd sense of detachment. He'd never seen a fire like it. The most common reasons for a fire like that would be because of an oil lamp spilled or someone being careless with a pipe. They were usually slow to start and rose up from the bottom. This one looked as though the roof had been set alight first. This fire had been deliberate, he was certain of it.

Miles splashed his face with water again and finally found the strength to come to his feet. "You had better clean yourself up and get some rest, lad," he told the stable hand, who had seemed mesmerized by the fire.

"I'll tend to the horses first," the boy vowed, hastening away.

As he stepped over to the house, feeling as though he had aged several decades, Mrs. Snow hurried out of the house and wrapped her arms around him once more.

"Mrs. Snow, I am filthy," he protested, his throat dry.

"We will forever be indebted to you." She stepped back and cupped his face in both hands. "She is well, if a little tired." Mrs.

Snow's brow furrowed. "You must come inside and have a drink and some rest."

He gestured to the barn. "It could not be saved."

She waved a hand. "Oh it is only a building. Now, come inside," she ordered.

He ducked into the drawing room. Now that he was away from the smoldering building, he could smell the smoke coming off of his clothes. He looked down to see he was leaving trails of soot. "Mrs. Snow..."

"Nothing that cannot be fixed." She tilted her head. "Do you need to lie down? Mr. Snow is resting or else he would be here to thank you too."

He cleared his throat. "I am well enough, Mrs. Snow. Please attend to your family."

She clasped her hands together. "The housekeeper is with Augusta at present but I should see that Mr. Snow is well..."

"Please do so but may I ask...that is, would you mind if I visit with Miss Snow—just to see that she is well for myself."

"Most certainly!"

Mrs. Snow led him upstairs and let him into Augusta's room. Laid against white sheets, she looked paler than ever. The smoke had been washed from her face and her skin was damp. Her eyes fluttered open and she bolted upright as soon as she saw him. "Miles!"

"Please do not—"

"I shall see to my husband, if you do not mind." She gave Miles's hand a squeeze. "Thank goodness you were nearby, Lord Ashwick. Whatever would we have done without you?"

He gave a tight smile but could not tear his gaze from Augusta. The housekeeper sat on a rocking chair in one corner, her hands folded across her stomach and her eyes shut. Even when Mrs. Snow departed the room, the woman did not open her eyes.

Augusta smiled. "It seems she has had a trying day."

"Not nearly as trying as you."

"Nor you." She reached for him and he could not resist taking those delicate fingers in his and coming to her bedside. "Mama says you saved my life."

He lifted his shoulders as he came to kneel beside the bed. "You saved the lives of those horses."

"It was Jenkins," she blurted out.

"Jenkins?"

"He was here. In my room. I..." She bit down on her bottom lip. "I hurt him and I'm certain he burned the barn in revenge."

"Christ," he muttered. "I shall ensure he is dealt with," he vowed.

"I know you will." She pressed the handkerchief she had bunched in one hand to her mouth when a coughing fit struck. Remaining sitting, she squeezed his hand tight. "Miles, I would have died in there had it not been for you—"

"Do not even say that," he said gruffly. He couldn't bear to think of anything happening to her.

"Miles, listen," she said with more force than he expected.

He let his lips curve. "Whatever you say, Miss Snow."

"I know that this is wrong to say and that given the circumstances with Henry...well...anyway, I must say this because all I could think about was how much I would regret it if I..."

He frowned. "Gus?"

"I love you," she blurted out.

Miles stared at her for several heartbeats. Had the smoke addled his wits? Surely she could not have...?

"I do not expect—"

Before she could say anything further, he rose and pressed a fierce kiss to her lips, silencing her. He shifted back to eye her, bringing a palm up to cup her cheek. She tilted her face so he could feel the cool softness of her skin.

"I love you, Gus," he said through a tight throat. "Damn it, woman, I love you more than you realize."

She beamed at him and he had to wonder if he had not died in that fire and gone to heaven. But that couldn't be right. He was not sure his tainted soul was ready for heaven yet. So this had to be real.

"I love you," she repeated softly.

A loud, abrupt snore from behind him prevented him saying anything further so he pressed a kiss to her forehead. "I'll make you mine," he vowed.

He wasn't sure how he was going to tell Henry about all this but now that he knew Augusta didn't love Henry...well, he had to do something. Somehow, he had to tell his brother the truth—that he had loved his fiancée for longer than he could remember.

Chapter Twenty-One

SKIRTS IN HAND, AUGUSTA stumbled along the groove worn into the grass by the passage of many hundreds of feet. Overhead, the sun shone intermittently through clouds as they moved swiftly across the sky. A breeze rippled the lengths of grass that spread out in front of her but she welcomed the slight chill it brought to her heated cheeks. If she thought too hard on this, she would turn around and return home and wait.

But no more.

No more waiting for life to happen to her. No more passively letting others make her decisions.

It had been two days since Miles had confessed his love for her and after a day's bed rest, she was itching to see him again. She was not certain why he had not visited since but she was simply done waiting.

The estate office was set on a winding farm track, a lone farm building with one cart parked outside. Her heart picked up its pace and she moved quicker. He had to be there. And with any luck, he might be alone.

Augusta approached the building slowly. Even if Miles' estate manager was there, she doubted he would have much to say about her being here alone—the man was hardly the sort for gossip—but she'd still rather avoid any scandal until she had spoken with Henry. Naturally, there would be talk that could not be avoided, and while the idea of being gossiped about once more made her toes curl into her boots, she knew it would be worth it. For the first time in her life, she was ready to take control of the direction in which she was headed.

She only hoped Miles still felt the same.

Stopping outside the red brick building, she peered in through the window. She ducked back swiftly when she saw Mr. Thomas, the estate manager, deep in conversation with Miles. At least she knew he was here, though. She had anticipated having to come up with an excuse to go to the house with her mother or perhaps asking Joanna to accompany her. How easy it would have been to talk to Miles alone there, she did not know, but she would do whatever it took.

Augusta slunk around the side of the building and waited, her back pressed against the rough brick. She squinted up at the sun as it touched her skin through a break in the clouds. With any luck, she would not have to wait long before catching Miles alone. He would have to leave eventually after all and she would probably dash after him and...

A door slammed shut and Augusta dashed around the corner, paused, and quickly retreated, ducking back behind the wall as Mr. Thomas left the building. She pressed a hand to her thudding chest and stole a glimpse around the building. If he had seen her, he showed no sign of it, continuing at a quick pace away from the office. She waited until he was some distance away before pressing open the front door and slipping inside the gloomy confines of the building.

Broken into several rooms, she could hear papers being shuffled to the right, where she had seen Miles. Swallowing the tight knot of half-excitement, half-nerves tightening her throat, she straightened her shoulders and stepped through the doorway into the main office. Miles was standing over a table, his brow creased in concentration while he riffled through paperwork. She took a moment to admire his bare hands, his fingers leafing through the sheets of paper confidently. She opened her mouth then shut it. It would be so easy to turn around, to wait and hope he would come and visit her. Surely he would? Her toes twitched with the desire to turn around and flee.

No more.

"Miles," she forced herself to say, his name rasping from her throat.

He turned swiftly, muttering a surprised curse under his breath. "Gus?"

She offered a shaky smile.

He glanced out of the window and moved past her to close the door and lock it. "What are you doing here?" He glanced her over. "You should still be resting. You should—"

She held up a hand. "I am perfectly fine."

Miles pushed a hand through his hair. "I was going to come and visit you but I thought—"

She could bear it no longer—looking at him and not being able to touch. The way he looked at her with such dark intensity, the heat that seemed to sizzle from his broad shoulders. It was too much. Taking two steps forward, she flung her arms around his neck and kissed him firmly, passionately.

A surprised sound rumbled up from him but it was only moments before his arms were wrapping around her waist, drawing her hard into him. He returned the kiss with what felt like as much built-up frustration as she had suffered. She savored the touch of his firm chest, molding against hers with a sigh. His fingers dug into her waist, just so, providing her all the support her now weak legs needed. She funneled her fingers through his hair, drinking in the freedom to touch him, to feel him, to take everything he had to offer.

When he broke away, every inch of her body felt heated and she gulped down a few breaths.

He kept her close, pressing his forehead briefly to hers before landing a chaste peck on her nose. "You should not be here," he murmured.

"I did not want to wait." She gave a light laugh. "I am very done with waiting."

"I know, forgive me." He eased back enough to view her properly. "I wanted to give you time to rest and...well, I was trying to figure out what to tell Henry."

"I think I should tell him. That is if..."

"I want you, Gus. More than anything." He lifted a shoulder. "Whatever happens, so long as I have you, I am not concerned."

She smiled, relieved. "I will speak with Henry as soon as I can."

"We shall do it together." He grimaced. "I hope he is not too upset."

Augusta gave a wry smile. "Somehow I think he will not be upset at all."

"You may be right, fool that he is." He cupped her face, his palms warm on her skin. "My only concern was you," he confessed. "I always thought Henry was what you wanted."

"For a brief while, perhaps he was, but I did not know my own mind." She returned his caress, smoothing a thumb along the slightly rough line of his jaw. "I do now, though."

"God, Gus, I thought I'd go mad with wanting you," he muttered before lowering his lips to hers.

She sighed at the contact, sinking into him and letting the waves of desire carry her along. His tongue delved, tasting her, sending flutters of delight swirling into her belly. She moved closer and shuddered at the feel of his firm body aligned so perfectly with hers. He groaned and shifted his hands down, down, down, following the curve of her spine, touching her hips then finally cupping her rear. His arousal prodded against her and she moaned into his mouth.

With a muttered curse, he lifted her. She latched her hands around his neck and her legs around his waist on instinct and a sound of delight escaped her. It took her a moment to realize it had even been her making such a noise. Her mind whirled, lost in a sea of need that had her desperate for more. Never in her lifetime could she have imagined such a moment. He pulled back briefly to meet her gaze and she saw the same emotion in him. His eyes were dark, his pupils wide. His breaths came raggedly and she felt the tension in his forearms as he battled for control. For the moment, she did not want him to have any.

"Miles," she whispered.

He responded with a firm kiss, his lips sealing over hers and delving deep once more. He staggered back a few steps then twisted around, bringing her down onto the desk. He shifted one hand down her leg, the other cradling her back so that she was angled just perfectly so.

"Oh!" she gasped between kisses.

He moved against her and sparks of pleasure burst behind her tightly closed eyelids. Tingles raced along every inch of her body. She grappled at his shoulders, digging her nails into his shirtsleeves. No wonder she had been so confused, so lost to him. Nothing had ever felt so right.

Miles shifted his mouth from hers, leaving her feeling briefly bereft. She opened her eyes as he trailed kisses down the arch of her throat. She shivered while new sensations rippled down her spine. He nibbled briefly at her ear, then kissed the hollow behind it. More open-mouthed kisses followed, moving down, down, down...

Her whole body ached with need and she arched into him. His mouth lingered over the subtle rise of her breasts then came back up to press firmly upon her mouth. He drew back and she opened her eyes to find him staring at her with more passion than she ever thought possible. She pressed a hand through his mussed hair.

"If you stay here any longer, I cannot guarantee I will remain a gentleman." He gave a gruff laugh and squeezed her leg. "Well, somewhat of a gentleman."

She sighed and blew out a breath. "I almost would rather you did not."

"We must speak with Henry first." He tapped her nose with a finger. "You know we must, Gus."

Biting down on her lip, she nodded. "I know."

Doubt flickered in his eyes. "You drive me to the edge of insanity, do you know that?"

"I think you are trying to do the same to me."

"I only hope I am doing the right thing by Henry. I owe my brother a lot."

"So you would consign me to a loveless marriage out of duty?"

He shook his head with a half-smile. "I am too selfish for that."

"I do not believe that."

"Ah, Gus, must you always believe the best of people." He ran his hands down her arms and took a step back.

"Only of you."

"I shall endeavor to spend the rest of my days trying to live up to your expectations. Exacting though they are."

She gave him a light tap on the arm. "Even now, you cannot help but tease me."

He lifted his shoulders. "Call it a habit." He aided her down from the desk but drew her straight into his arms once more, holding her close and running his gaze over her face. "I look forward to having the freedom to hold you like this whenever I wish."

"Me too."

"But for now, you had better return home."

"And we shall tell Henry tomorrow?"

Miles shook his head. "Wednesday. I do not expect him to return from wherever he is until then."

Two days. She could survive that she supposed. At least it would give her time to summon the words to explain to Henry what she felt. It was not going to be an easy road—breaking an engagement with one brother only to become engaged to another. No doubt it would invite some awful salacious gossip. She peered into Miles's intense gaze and smiled. It would be worth it, of that she was certain.

Chapter Twenty-Two

"LORD ASHWICK, THERE is a...man here to see you."

Miles peered over his paper and scowled. "A man?" Why had his butler not taken his name? Or perhaps Greggs had and Miles simply had not noticed. He could not help but feel distracted considering his brother was due to return tomorrow and Augusta planned to visit so they could tell him the truth.

"Show him into the drawing room," Miles said, folding the paper.

Greggs shook his head, tightening his lips. "I have him in the kitchen. It seems the best place for him."

Miles's frown deepened but he shrugged. "Very well." If it was one of the tenant farmers, they'd not be happy simply being left in the kitchen thanks to muddy boots but hopefully Miles could smooth over any issues.

Rising from the breakfast table, he made his way quickly downstairs and through the dim corridors to the kitchen. Lit by thin windows high up by the ceiling and not receiving the sun on this side yet, the room was gloomy—and empty. Apparently, his guest had scared all the maids away. He slowed his pace once his eyes had adjusted to the dim light and the silhouette of the man became apparent. His back was to him but Miles would recognize those shoulders and posture anywhere.

Nester turned with a grin. "Lord Ashwick." He removed his hat and performed a ridiculous bow.

"What the bloody hell are you doing here?" Miles curled a fist at his side.

"I told you I'd not forgotten about you."

"I don't give a fig. What makes you think you can step inside my house?"

"Well, I was invited in." He grinned. "Though, I had rather hoped I might get an invite into the posh rooms. I even wore my best hat." He shook the article of clothing in question at him.

Jaw tight, Miles forced a breath through his teeth. The old man was as manipulative as any man could get but Miles was no longer an impressionable young man, looking for a use for his fists. "I suggest you leave, Nester, before I set my gamekeeper on you. He's an excellent shot." Miles paused. "As am I. And you are trespassing."

Nester's grin expanded. "See? You're still the same old Stanton. No title can change that. Always ready with a threat."

"So you should know well enough that I always follow through on my threats."

The old man took a few steps toward him, skirting around the long table that ran down the center of the kitchen. The stench of stale alcohol and smoke grew stronger. "Come on, Miles, we both know you must be bored out of your wits. This isn't you." He gestured around the room. "You might have been born to money but we both know the blood of a scoundrel runs through your veins."

"Not anymore," Miles said tightly.

"Think of what we could achieve with your new powers and my wiles. You'd never have a dull day."

"You really believe you are offering me something, do you not?" Miles shook his head. "You always were addled but age has done you no good."

"I'm offering you safety."

Miles chuckled. "You think you scare me, old man."

"No, but I might scare that pretty lady of yours just like I did your brother."

Heat roared through his veins. He stepped forward and grabbed Nester by the scruff of his shirt, slamming him down onto the kitchen table. The old man struggled for a moment then relaxed, laughing.

"See? You haven't changed a bit."

"What do you know of her?"

"I know you like to spend time with her alone." He tugged at Miles's hand as Miles pressed harder, making the man's face redden. "Time kissing. On tables, for example." He laughed, the sound gruff and cracked. "You should have just taken her then and there. Now you'll never get the chance."

The heat inside him chilled to sudden ice. His heart dropped down to his toes. "What do you mean?" Miles asked hoarsely.

"Come join me. Then you can be sure nothing will happen to those you care about again."

Miles eased his grip on him and allowed him to stand. "Where. Is. She?" he demanded.

Nester shrugged, straightening his shirt. "Could be anywhere." His grin turned wicked. "If you would just help me with one thing, I'm certain I can find out for you."

Miles stared at him. There was no way he could go back. Whatever Nester was involved in, it would hurt people. It may have already hurt Augusta. "Go to hell," he muttered.

"Stanton..."

His fist struck flesh before he'd even registered it. Blood exploded from Nester's face. Miles cradled his sore knuckles while the man cursed and cupped his nose. "It's Lord Ashwick to you," he bit out. "And I'm excellent friends with the local magistrate. I can be sure to have you put away for threatening a member of the aristocracy and trespassing." He closed the gap between them once more, forcing the man against the wall. "Unless you tell me where the woman is."

"I told you, I don't know."

Miles grabbed him by his shirt neck again and hauled him into the silverware room. Shoving him in, Miles slammed the door against his protests and locked it from the outside. Pocketing the key, he marched upstairs. "Have word sent to the local jail. A thief and trespasser is locked in the silverware room," he told Greggs.

"My-my lord?"

"I need to leave. Now. Just get someone here."

Miles didn't wait for a response and snatched one of the horses that had been saddled for exercise. He had to find Augusta before anything happened to her. Damn him and damn his past. If it weren't for his idiotic behavior as a young man, she would never be threatened. He rode hard toward the Snows' house, cutting across fields while his mind raced.

Hell's teeth, he'd never forgive himself if she was harmed. He should have known seeing Nester again would bring trouble. The man likely could not resist Miles's new wealth and connections. What a fool he was to think he could put his past behind him and pretend to be an upstanding viscount worthy of a woman like Augusta.

He rode out to Augusta's house, his shaking fingers pulling the doorbell. Neither Augusta or her parents were home and the housekeeper could not say where Augusta had gone, only that she was with Mrs. Lockhart and Miss Larkin. He cursed softly under his breath and forced himself to offer a polite farewell before riding his horse into town.

If she was with the two women, she was vulnerable. As much as her friends seemed loyal, there was little they could do against the sort of men Nester had under his command. He frantically hunted through every shop and tea shop but there was no sign of any of them.

Where the devil were they? Walking? Visiting with each other? God damn it, if Nester had hurt Augusta, he'd tear the man to shreds rather than waiting for the law to deal with him.

He stomped out of the tea shop and tugged his pocket watch out. Two hours had passed since Nester had come to his house. He could be too late. She could already be—

No, he couldn't think of such a thing happening to her. The chances were they would hold her for ransom—it was not unknown for them to do so. But what would she suffer in the meantime? He mounted his horse and led her out toward Mrs.

Lockhart's house. Hopefully someone would know what had happened to them.

As he rode a frantic pace down the lane, an open carriage, driven by a woman by the looks of it, trundled down the road. Both occupants of the vehicles wore bonnets. His heart thudded so hard against his ribs that it made his gut roll. It had to be her, surely?

Picking up the pace, he caught up with the vehicle, calling Augusta's name. The carriage drew to a halt and he stopped by the side of it, catching a glimpse of dark hair under the bonnet of the passenger. Mrs. Lockhart scowled. "Lord Ashwick, whatever is the matter?"

He ignored her, looking to Augusta. "You are well? Unharmed?"

Augusta's brow puckered. "Yes, but—"

"No one threatened you?"

She shook her head. "Miles, is all well? You look terribly—"

"Are you certain?" he demanded. "There was no one following you? No one you did not recognize?"

"We had a lovely tea at Miss Larkins while we discussed wedding plans, then we strolled around her fiancés grounds," Mrs. Lockhart said. "We have not been threatened or followed, I can assure you of that."

Augusta put a hand to Mrs. Lockhart's arm and climbed from the carriage. Miles dismounted deftly off his horse and strode around the vehicle to meet her, taking hold of her arms and looking her over. "You are certain you are well?"

"Yes, perfectly fine. What is the matter, Miles? You look frightful."

"Because I thought—" Miles shook his head. Of course Nester wouldn't be foolish enough to take Augusta. He was a terrible person but he was no fool. Abducting a local woman would draw far too much attention. He must have hoped the mere threat would be enough to get Miles to act.

And it almost had been.

"Miles, what has happened?" she asked softly.

He cast his gaze over her, drinking in her wide eyes and soft lips, remembering how they felt against his own. "Nothing has happened."

"This does not look like nothing." She gestured to his bedraggled appearance.

"Nothing that concerns you, Gus, I promise you. I thought it did but I was wrong."

"If you are upset, then I think it—"

"No," he barked. "It does not concern you. It never should have." He cursed under his breath. "I was a fool to think I could have you."

"What on earth do you mean?"

He grimaced and rubbed a hand over his face, feeling the stubble that he'd yet to remove that day. "You'd be better off with Henry," he muttered.

"Miles?" Hurt flickered in her eyes. "You cannot be serious..."

"I am." He gave a wry laugh. "I really am."

"No." She shook her head and crossed her arms.

"He's the better brother, Gus."

"No," she repeated firmly.

"Gus, damn it."

"Whatever the problem is, we can deal with it together."

"That is the trouble," he said, "you cannot deal with it. You should not have to. It's my rotten past and it should never be inflicted upon you."

She tilted your head. "This is about your past?"

He nodded stiffly, wishing to God she did not look so damned beautiful and sweet. Her friend kept her gaze pointedly forward but no doubt Mrs. Lockhart could hear every word. He took Augusta's arm and led her a little further away. "I thought it was behind me but it is not. It never will be."

"All men are a little wild in their youth. All that matters is the man you are now."

He snorted. "I am no different. I wish I was for you, but I'm not. I cannot have you being placed in danger."

"Why would I be in danger, Miles? You are not making any sense!"

"Look, I was a bad person in my youth. It was not some mere rakish behavior. I did bad things, hurt good people."

She bit down on her bottom lip. "I thought it was just some drinking, maybe some gambling."

He shook his head. "I spent time with people who would think nothing of slicing your throat for some jewels. And I stood by and let it all happen."

"But—"

"Listen to me, Gus." He gripped both arms tightly, forcing her to look at him. "Henry is the brother you want, not me."

She lifted her chin. "You cannot tell me what I want."

"I can, and it's not me." Miles released her arms and turned away, swiftly mounting his horse without looking at her. "It's not me," he told her once more. "I wish to hell it was and I'm more sorry than you can imagine, but it's not me."

She opened her mouth but no response came. Miles didn't wait for her to summon any words but he could feel her gaze upon his back as he rode away. Clenching the reins tightly, he willed himself to keep his gaze ahead. He wasn't wrong, but first he had to do one more thing for her. If he was going to make sure she was truly safe, he needed to pay Jenkins a visit. If he was going to use his past for anything good, he'd remind the man exactly who he really was.

Chapter Twenty-Three

"ARE YOU QUITE WELL?" Joanna asked, taking Augusta's hands in hers as Augusta greeted her and Chloe on the doorstep of the family home.

Augusta managed a tiny nod. She glanced at Chloe, who gave her a sympathetic smile. It seemed Joanna had apprised her of the situation with Miles. After he approached them two days ago, shaken and upset, Augusta had no choice but to confess all to Joanna. She could not claim to feel much better but she had at least come to a firm decision...

Regardless of what had happened between her and Miles, she could not marry Henry. It was not fair to him and it was not fair to her. For the first time in her life, she was going to make a decision for herself, regardless of what their families might think, regardless of what the future may hold for her.

"Thank you for coming," she said, her voice hoarse.

She had cried herself ragged yesterday but had awoken with a strange sense of strength today. She supposed she had been feeling it grow since the moment she'd decided to cease awaiting Henry's return but it had blossomed overnight, somehow born of her frustration and heartbreak at Miles's confusing behavior. Why did he think she cared for his past? Why did he let it haunt him so?

Well, if she could do nothing about him, she could at least do something about her fiancé.

"I was hoping you might take me to Charlecote House." Augusta gave a hopeful smile.

"Oh?" Joanna's brows lifted. "To see Miles? Or Henry?"

"Henry," she replied.

"We will do whatever you need us to do, is that not right, Chloe?" Joanna looked to Chloe.

She nodded firmly. "Including giving that Lord Ashwick a piece of my mind if I need to."

Augusta's smile widened. "That will not be necessary, I promise."

"Well, let us get on our way." Joanna gestured to the carriage, awaiting them on the road.

Ignoring her shaking hands and the nerves swirling in her belly, Augusta settled on the seat next to Chloe, aware that both of her friends were watching her as they went on their way. She wished she could tell them more but, if she was honest, she had hardly considered quite what was going to happen when she'd penned a quick note to her friends, asking for their help. If she went with her mother, there was no chance she could speak with Henry honestly.

And today was a day for complete honesty, for the first time in a long time.

"What if Lord Ashwick is at home?" Chloe asked. "Surely you have no desire to see him?"

Augusta shook her head. "He will not be. He, um, is usually at the estate offices at this time."

Heat rose in her cheeks when she recalled her last visit there. It would be something she'd never forget. She bit back a sigh. If only she could fathom what had been running through Miles's head...if only she could come up with some way of fixing the situation. But she was at a loss. He had seemed so determined, so anguished. It had taken a good deal of strength to even drag herself out of bed today let alone contemplate whether there was some way of reassuring him that she did not care for his past. Even if it did seem it was far more awful than she had realized...

"Chloe and I may take a walk around the ground before joining you, if you do not mind," Joanna suggested when they drew up outside of the house.

"Or we can stay with you, if you prefer," Chloe offered quickly.

Augusta felt herself blanch as the reality of what she was to do struck hard. Regardless, she shook her head. "No. I should do this alone."

Joanna gave her hand a little squeeze before they disembarked and went their separate directions. Augusta straightened her spine and climbed the steps to the front door on shaky legs. She was led to the drawing room and only had to wait a few moments until Henry joined her. He smiled, flashing white teeth at her. She could not help but smile back. Once upon a time, that smile would have sent her belly tumbling over itself, but that easily swayed young girl was long gone.

"What a pleasure to see you, Augusta. You will have to forgive my recent absences, I was—"

August held up a hand. "I need to say something, if you do not mind," she said hastily. Any longer and she would lose her courage.

Both brows rose but he nodded. "Of course." He gestured to one of the seats in the elegant gold and red room but she remained standing. Hands clasped in front of her, she drew in a long breath. "I...I wish to break off the engagement."

He blinked at her several times and silence fell over the room. The chitter of a bird and the humming of a maid somewhere were the only sounds. Several ticks of a clock went by. Henry rubbed his forehead with a finger. "If this is because of my behavior, then please be assured—"

"No, it is because of mine."

"Yours?"

She nodded. "I love another." There. It was said. And, goodness, how good it felt. She loosened her hands and lifted her chin. "I'm sorry, Henry. I believe our engagement was a mistake and that you do not want me for a wife any more than I want you."

He pinched the bridge of his nose. "Our families will be most upset."

"But will you be?"

He smiled vaguely. "I am afraid to say I will not."

"Do not be afraid. I think fear is what got us both in this position."

He nodded and chuckled. "I think so too." He gestured again to one of the chairs. "Please sit, Augusta," he insisted.

She relented and perched on a high-backed red velvet sofa.

Henry seated himself opposite, leaning forward with his elbows upon his knees. "You are certain about this?"

"I am." She tilted her head and eyed him. "You do not seem all that surprised."

His lips curved. "I had rather picked up on some reluctance on your part, and shall we say...some feelings toward another person."

Augusta sucked in a breath. No, how could he possibly know?

"It is Miles, is it not?"

She stilled, unable to fathom a response.

"When we were younger, I always had an inkling you rather liked Miles."

"I liked you too," she protested.

"But not as much as Miles, and I would wager he likes you immensely. Always has, I suppose. If I'd have realized it sooner, I might not have been such a fool about this whole thing."

"Whole thing?"

He grimaced and rubbed a hand over his face. "I was wrong to propose in the first place but I was also wrong to leave you. And then..."

"Then?"

"I fell in love."

"Love?" she echoed.

He blew out a breath. "I met a woman in Hungary—Gizella." His eyes warmed at the mention of her name. "I fell in love with her but I knew nothing could come of it. Not just because I could not break our engagement and ruin you but because she is poor, with no connections." He shook his head. "Could you imagine how my family would be should I break things off with you and bring home a poor Hungarian?"

Augusta bit down on her lip. "I was rather hoping not to disappoint my family too, but, Henry, you have a loving family, as do I. They will want the best for us."

"Even when we tell them you have ended things, they shall want me to look for a nice society girl. At least if you marry Miles, your family shall be quite content."

Tears bit into the corners of her eyes suddenly and she swiped them away.

"Augusta?"

"I do not think that will happen anyway. He...he does not want anything to do with me." She stared at her hands. "Something about his past."

"That damned fool," he muttered. "I have no idea why he thinks he should be haunted by it so. He's determined to pay penance until the end of his days."

"Was it really so bad?"

"It was," Henry confirmed. "He was involved with some very dangerous people. So much so that I unfortunately ended up in a little trouble."

"Trouble?" she echoed.

"He made some enemies and I received something of a beating when I refused to talk of Miles. Suffice to say, my brother is still riddled with guilt over the matter, despite it being years ago."

"I had no idea."

"But Miles is a good man, you know that or else you would not have fallen for him."

"No," she agreed. "I would not have."

"He will come around."

"I am not so sure." She forced a smile. "But what of your lady friend? You should go back to Hungary and bring her here."

He glanced down. "I am ashamed to say I have already done so."

"Oh."

"I had every intention of being faithful to you, Augusta, I promise. I just wanted to ensure she had a good life. Unfortunately, getting her settled here was harder than I anticipated. Hence, why I did not attend the ball. She ended up in rather a pickle with her landlord and I had to make assurances."

She grimaced. "Poor woman. I cannot imagine being alone in a new country."

"Gizella is a resourceful woman but it has not been easy, that much is true."

"Well, you should make it easier on her."

"I cannot."

Augusta rose from her seat and Henry's gaze followed her. "You know you have been quite a coward in your attitude toward me, Henry. I should like to think you have learned from it."

"I know, I know."

"No, you do not know. You left me waiting for a long time and I wish both of us had summoned the courage to speak up sooner."

"But—"

"Henry, marry Gizella. You know it is the right thing to do."

He shook his head and grinned. "You were always so quiet, Augusta, whatever happened to you?"

She lifted her shoulders. "Love, I suppose."

Chapter Twenty-Four

MILES SCOWLED AT THE clear sky, almost annoyed that the day should be so nice. At least if it was raining, it would match his sullen mood. Henry rode beside him, muttering something about the weather but Miles wasn't paying attention. The truth was, he had not paid attention to much since the other day, when he'd sent Augusta away. He ground his teeth together, recalling her hurt, confused look. His heart gave a sharp jab at his ribs.

"So, I hear tell that you had a little word with Jenkins."

The name caught Miles's attention and he turned to face his brother. "How did you hear about that?"

"It is not often a man pisses his breeches and runs away to goodness knows where." Henry chuckled. "You really must have scared the man."

"Let's just say I reminded him of exactly who I once was then threw in a few threats of suing for slander."

"I heard he was behind those rumors."

Miles said nothing and kept his expression blank. He wasn't aware Henry had been around enough to hear of the gossip about him and Augusta. They rode leisurely along the path that led down to the river that cut across much of Hampshire. Miles knew he should have declined the ride but his brother was beginning to get suspicious about his melancholy mood so he'd relented.

"I also heard he was suspected to be behind the fire at the Snows."

"That much is true," Miles confirmed.

"And the rumors?" his brother pressed.

Miles tightened his jaw and fixed his gaze on the bank of trees that followed the line of the stream. He couldn't lie to his brother but he'd be damned if he'd get in the way of Augusta and Henry.

"You know, I saw Augusta two days ago," his brother continued.

Sighing, Miles looked to Henry. His brother was not going to make this ride as relaxing as Miles had hoped. "I did not know."

"Yes, it was rather interesting." Henry grinned. "She's changed quite a bit since I first proposed."

"Indeed."

"And, of course, she told me she could not marry me."

Miles nearly choked on a breath. "She told you—"

"She could not marry me, yes. Seems she's in love with someone else."

"I—" Miles eased his grip on the reins, aware his tension was putting his horse on edge. "And you are not upset?"

"Of course not. We both know I only proposed out of grief and the weight of expectation. Thankfully she was clever and brave enough to put a stop to it."

"Good Lord..." Miles murmured.

"There was also the matter of, well, the fact that I am also in love with someone else."

"Damn it, were you having an affair?"

Henry grimaced. "I did not intend to."

Miles's teeth began to hurt from all the grinding.

Henry held up a hand. "I met someone when I was in the Baltics. I brought her home with me—"

"Henry," Miles growled.

"But I did not have relations with her!" his brother protested. "I simply wanted to ensure she had a better life. I have her set up in a comfortable house now."

"Bloody hell, Henry, you do not do things easily, do you?"

"She was desperately poor, Miles. I could not leave her behind, even when I decided I needed to do the right thing by Augusta."

Absorbing the information, he took in his brother's appearance. Henry appeared more relaxed than he had done since his return. "So this woman? What are you going to do with her?"

"Marry her, hopefully." Henry uttered the words quietly.

"Does she have any connections?"

"None at all."

Miles shook his head. "Mother will have a fit."

"And you?"

"If you love her, you have my support."

Henry's shoulders dropped. "Good. Excellent. You shall adore her, I promise. She's quiet but strong...rather like Augusta."

He wished his brother would stop mentioning her. Though, he had to wonder, why had she broke things off? She had everything she needed in Henry—protection, wealth, looks, not to mention everyone loved Henry. That didn't change—

His pulse came to a juddering halt at the sight of the tall, slender woman by the riverside. Her feet were bare, her skirts slightly lifted and she was dipping her toes in the water. For a moment, he'd thought it was Augusta but it could not be. She would never be so close to the water's edge.

Damn it all, now he was going addled.

"I asked her to meet me here so we could discuss telling everyone of the broken engagement," Henry said.

Miles twisted to view his brother, frowning.

"Augusta," Henry explained, "I asked her to meet me here."

Miles turned his attention back to the woman. Of course it was her. There was no one else who made his stomach twist and his skin heat as though he was standing by a furnace with just one glance. But what the devil was she doing?

"Well, I had better leave you," Miles said tightly.

Henry shook his head. "I think *I* should leave you."

"Henry?"

"I wanted to see it for myself and now I have. You love that woman, Miles, and she certainly loves you."

"But—"

His brother grinned. "Whatever or whoever you were in the past, you have proven yourself more than capable of protecting her. Hell, protecting all of us. Have you not provided for and protected me from my foolish decisions all these years?"

"But you were hurt, Henry."

"I was but I can see you have no inclination of letting that happen to Augusta." Henry jerked his head toward her. "Go to her."

Miles hesitated. Every fiber of his being was pulling toward her but he wasn't certain he could dampen that voice inside him that told him he was not good enough for her.

"Go, Miles, or I shall force you."

Nodding curtly, Miles directed his horse down toward the riverside, dismounting and tethering the reins to a strong branch. He waited for a moment, tucked just behind the tree, and watched while she dipped her toes into the water. Her shoes and stockings were discarded to one side and he smiled, despite himself. Augusta was so much more courageous than either of them had realized.

"Gus," he said finally, the word rasping in his throat.

She spun, skirts in hand. "Oh!" She dropped them quickly, smoothing her palms down her crinkled gown. "Miles!"

He took a few steps toward her, unable to keep the quirked smile from his face. It had been mere days and he'd missed her so damned much. He fisted his hands at his sides to prevent from taking her straight into his arms.

She glanced around him. "I was meant to be meeting Henry here."

"Henry decided to go home."

Creases appeared on her brow. "Oh?"

He drew in a long breath. "It seems my brother intended for us to meet. He told me he wanted my company for a ride."

"Ah." She bit down on her bottom lip and fingered the fabric of her skirt.

Miles closed the distance between them and glanced at the bare toes peeking out from under the lemon-yellow hem. "You hate water."

"I do." She lifted her chin. "But I'm brave now."

"I can see that." He eyed her, taking in the determined point of her chin and the wide, dark eyes that were, for the first time in a while, without makeup. God, he wanted her more than ever and he wasn't certain he could deny himself. "Henry said you broke off the engagement."

"He did not love me and I do not love him. I do not think he was upset by it at all."

"No, I do not think so either."

"Miles—"

"Gus—" He paused and tried again. "Gus...I am no perfect man."

"I do not think you are."

He chuckled. "You are so good for one's ego, Miss Snow."

"I am not perfect either. We would be fools to think we were. I considered Henry perfect once and look where that led me."

"I suppose you are right, though you shall have a hard time convincing me you are not the most perfect woman in the world."

"My hair is too dark."

He fingered a curl, tracing the path of it down her neck. A tiny tremor wracked her body. "This hair is perfect."

"I am too slender."

Miles moved closer, spanning both hands around her waist. "Your body is perfect."

"I am too shy, and scared, and...and foolish."

"You are never too anything, Gus." He drew her into him, muttering the words against the skin of her neck. "Apart from too perfect." He lifted his head before he could give into temptation and flatten his lips to her skin. "I, however, am a fool. The biggest one there ever was."

"I..." She sank into him and pressed her head into his neck. "Lord, I missed you, Miles."

"My past is dark, Gus. I cannot deny I am still scared for you."

"Then we can both be scared. And hopefully, we can both gain courage." She lifted her head and smiled at him. "Besides, you've saved my life twice now. I think I am perfectly safe in your hands."

He groaned at the idea of her truly in his hands, her flesh filling his palms. "I find it impossible to deny you."

"Then do not." She lifted on tiptoes to press her lips to his.

Growling, he took what was offered, holding her firmly to him and sealing his mouth over hers. Any thoughts of denying himself fled. He kissed her until she was breathless and his arousal ached agonizingly. He tore away and eyed her flushed cheeks, drawing the back of a finger down one. "Your family shall have a bit of a shock when we tell them you have broken it off with Henry."

"Perhaps."

"And are now engaged to me."

"Is that a proposal?"

"A terrible one, yes."

She grinned. "I have had better, I shall admit."

"Damn that brother of mine and damn your exacting standards, Gus." He pressed a light kiss to her lips.

"My standards are not so exacting."

"Or else you would not be with me."

"That is not what I was going to say." She wriggled in his hold. "Why must you always tease me so?"

He kept her held firmly into his grasp until she gave up with an exasperated sigh. "If I promise not to tease, will you say yes?"

"I do not think you have the ability to cease teasing."

"Will you say yes anyway?"

She sank back into him and looped her arms around his neck. "Of course I will."

Miles could not keep the foolish grin from his face. "You know, we are not all that far from the estate office."

"Oh?"

"I recall making some rather fine memories there."

"So do I."

"It will be nice and quiet there."

She unlooped her arms from around his neck and snatched up her boots and stockings before slipping her hand in his. "Lead the way, Lord Ashwick. I do not think I am done being brave for the day."

THE END

www.samanthaholtromance.com

READ ON FOR A SAMPLE CHAPTER OF *THERE ARE PLENTY MORE DUKES IN THE SEA*

Chapter One

LONDON, 1818

Angel inched open the door, breath held. Her heart pressed against the bodice of her gown. Perhaps, just perhaps, if she stepped into the room quietly, no one would notice the late hour. The door hinge squeaked, and she winced.

Blast.

Easing one slippered foot through the tiny entrance she'd created, she crept through the gap into her brother's office. The fair heads of her siblings remained focused on the lawyer who sat facing Angel. The slender man, his gray hair pasted over a balding and splotchy scalp, did not look up.

She let loose a breath and immediately regretted it as the sound seemed to fill the quiet room. Her oldest brother, the Marquis of Eastbrook, gave her the briefest of glances. A lone brow arched. Angel felt her very soul shrivel. Theo was infamous for his stony glares, and she had been on the receiving end of them one too many times.

A smile stretched across her lips. She took a few sideways steps and slipped into the chair next to her mother. The gilded chair gave a little creak when she relaxed into it, and she grimaced. Angel kept her smile in place then glanced at her siblings. Even Seth had a stern expression fixed to his face.

Blast.

She released the smile and pressed her lips into a stern line of aloofness. Lord, the corners of her lips itched to curve already, and her brows felt weighted and unnatural. It was not that she was not deeply sorry their grandfather had passed—the man had doted on them all and had been one of the funniest, sweetest men she had ever known—but there was only so long one could grieve. And frankly, grieving was a messy business, and she did not much fancy partaking in it. Far better to thrust one's chin up and get on with things in her opinion. She was certain that was the way Grandpapa would have wanted it.

"You are late," her mother whispered while the lawyer shuffled a few papers.

"Well, you see...there was a problem with my hair. And then I saw Miss Newhurst as I was about to leave, and naturally I could not be rude. *And* there was trouble with my carriage..." She clamped her mouth shut when her mother arched an eyebrow.

Angel peered at the graying brow. So that was where her brother had learned it. Why had she not spotted that before? Perhaps because their Mama was a soft sort of character and rarely scolded any of them, especially not Angel, the youngest of them all.

Minerva at least spared her a brief smile before turning her attention back to the lawyer. Her sister wore her mourning wear with more confidence than she had ever worn a fine gown of lace and silk. The gray gown was formless and frightful, but Angel had never seen her older sister look more comfortable. Minerva was so shy and retiring that she probably adored how it failed to draw a single jot of attention.

Angel fingered her own gray gown. It would not be long before she could return to wearing bright colors and fine fabrics. She could hardly wait. Gray did not go well with her pale complexion and brought out the darkness under her eyes. The rest of her siblings and even her mother did much better in dark colors than her thanks to their fair hair and alabaster skin. Angel's own mahogany brown hair looked its best when coiled artfully over a sheath of vibrant silk.

The lawyer cleared his throat, and Angel lifted her gaze. A thin sheen of sweat covered the man's forehead, and he licked his lips, making Angel frown. Mr. Barton had worked for the family for as long as she could recall and had no reason to be nervous. Her brother might be one of the more powerful men in the country and had a countenance that could frighten many a man, but she could not fathom why Mr. Barton appeared so nervous.

"Well, now that we are all here, shall we begin?" he asked, looking to Theo.

Theo gave a stiff nod. "If you please."

The lawyer tweaked his cravat and pushed spindly glasses back up his nose. "As you are aware, your grandfather had no sons and there are no male relatives to inherit."

Angel looked away from the lawyer's sweaty features. Their grandfather had been a baron of excellent means thanks to some fine investments. Why that meant all of them needed to gather, she did not know. With no male heirs, it was assumed most of the wealth would pass to their mother—his only daughter—and maybe Theo as the oldest grandchild. Goodness knows, Angel would far rather be joining Miss Newhurst at Hyde Park and enjoying the fine weather while trying to spot the Duke of Norwick, who was known to drive his curricle through the park on warm days like today. Though she was not certain she wanted him seeing her in such grim clothes. He would never fall at her feet in this unattractive sack of a dress.

Fixing her attention back onto Mr. Barton, she pressed herself to listen. Did the man have to have such a droning voice? It was horribly difficult to concentrate on his words when he spoke in that monotonous tone.

"My daughter will inherit a sum of one thousand a year for the rest of her natural life and my beloved family home—Holbury Hall." Mr. Barton glanced up, presumably to look for her mother's reaction, but she remained a mask of dignity even though Angel knew her mother would be glad that the home where they had all enjoyed such wonderful childhood memories was hers.

Mr. Barton licked his lips and drew out a handkerchief to dab his forehead. "And finally, I, George Lockett, decree that my grandchildren, herein named, will inherit the rest of my fortune in its entirety, so long as they fulfill the following terms."

Angel drew her attention from the pretty gilding that ran along the edge of the room and shared a look with Seth, who made a face and gave a shrug. None of them had anticipated inheriting anything from Grandpapa, but the Templetons could certainly do with the funds. After their brother had been swindled by his late-wife, they all had vowed to take as little as possible from him, but it was not easy to live on little as Angel had discovered.

"Each person must complete their task to my lawyer's satisfaction or their share of the inheritance shall be forfeit," Mr. Barton continued.

The man glanced around the room. Angel's siblings remained still, brows creased. Minerva pursed her lips and opened her mouth before shutting it again. Theo tugged his jacket straight. Seth leaned in then shifted back in his chair.

Angel huffed. It would always be up to her to speak up for them all, which was ridiculous. She was the youngest for goodness sakes, but they were all too held up by the idea of propriety—even Seth, who prided himself on being quite the rake.

She held up a finger. "Mr. Barton, if I may, what on earth do you mean by 'task'? And to whom will the money be forfeit?"

The lawyer shifted in his seat and scanned the paper in front of him. "I was just...um...about to get to that."

"Well...?" Angel pressed.

"Angel," her mama hissed.

Chastened, Angel folded her arms across her chest and tapped a finger against an arm.

"Let's see." Mr. Barton's brow puckered. "Ah."

"What is it?" Theo asked, a hint of irritation edging his voice.

Angel noted *he* did not get scolded by their mother.

"If you are unable to fulfill your tasks to my satisfaction, all remaining inheritance shall be bestowed upon a Mr. Hastings."

A sharp inhale of breath echoed around the room. Angel met Minerva's worried gaze.

"That's preposterous," Theo blurted.

"Theo," Mama scolded.

Angel had no time to be smug that her brother had finally been reproached. How could she celebrate such a tiny achievement when the bulk of their wonderful Grandpapa's wealth could go to such a beast of a man?

"What the devil was Grandfather thinking?" murmured Seth.

Minerva shook her head. "This cannot be right. He would never give his money to that man."

Mr. Barton lifted his shoulders. "The will is quite clear. Should you fail, Mr. Hastings shall inherit."

"He is not even family," Theo said, his tone bitter.

Especially not after he separated from their cousin and brought utter scandal upon their family when he tried to gain a divorce and ran off with a nursemaid to Ireland. As far as they were all concerned, Mr. Hastings had not been part of the family for a good five years and their grandpapa had been suitably riled at the whole sorry mess. It was unfathomable that he should inherit anything after what he'd done to their poor cousin who passed away only six months after the event.

"You said there were tasks, correct?" Seth leaned back in his chair and waved a hand. "We'll do whatever it is that Grandfather wanted of us, and that will be the end of the matter."

Mr. Barton's dimpled cheeks reddened. "Well, ah, the instructions are extremely specific. All four grandchildren must complete their tasks within two months of this reading."

Seth gave a smug shrug. "Easy enough."

"For you perhaps," said Theo. "You have few commitments."

"And I had volunteered to help Lady Whitbury reorganize her library. I can hardly back out now," cried Minerva.

Angel rolled her eyes. As if her sister needed yet another excuse to be buried in books. It would do her good to do something different, of that Angel was certain. "I am sure she will survive without you, Minnie."

"But—"

Mama lifted both hands. "Perhaps we should find out what these tasks are before we leap to conclusions."

Theo straightened in his seat. "Quite. Yes. Mr. Barton, what exactly did our grandfather want of us?"

"There are letters for all of you..." Mr. Barton lifted a stack of letters. "Each describes your task." He handed them out.

Angel eyed her name written in her grandpapa's slightly shaky handwriting and her throat tightened. She swallowed the knot and turned it over to press a finger under the seal.

"But before you do." The lawyer dabbed his forehead again before thrusting his handkerchief back up a sleeve. "You must understand that no one can know of your task. The only people who may be privy to your task are the people in this room, including me. I will, ah, assess whether or not it is felt you have completed your undertaking."

"So we can discuss this with each other?" Theo clarified.

Mr. Barton nodded. "And your lady mother. But no one else."

"Well, let us get this thing done and then we can ensure that awful man does not get a penny of Grandpapa's fortune." Minerva flicked open her letter and scanned the contents.

Angel watched her sister's brow pucker then her mouth drop open. Her skin turned a strange ashen cast.

"What is it, Min?" Seth demanded.

"I..." She waved the letter at Seth. "Perhaps you should open yours."

Seth rolled his eyes. "You do not need to be scared of everything, Min. How bad can it be?"

Angel allowed herself a smile. Whatever was in the letter could not be that bad. After all, Minerva was terrified of most things. She spent most of her time reading or writing and spending time with a limited few friends. Anything out of the ordinary practically petrified her.

"Bloody hell," Seth murmured.

"Seth!" their mother scolded.

With a heavy stomach, Angel glanced at her own letter. What could these letters contain that would shock even Seth? Her senior by two years, Seth had been playing the rake for enough time to have experienced most of what life had to offer. He was the most fun sibling, and she utterly adored spending time with him, even if he did occasionally take his role of rake a little too far. Angel had thought him impervious to shock.

"Theo?" Angel nodded to the unopened letter in his hand.

His shoulders dropped, and he pulled out a penknife to work open the seal. His lips compressed into a thin line.

"Will no one tell me what theirs say?" Angel asked.

Her siblings ignored her. Her mother tapped her hand. "Perhaps you should open yours, dear."

Aware of her hands shaking slightly, Angel ripped open the letter, ignoring Theo's disapproving glare of the mess she made of the letter. This was ridiculous. Why was she so terrified of the contents of this letter? Was she not Lady Angel Templeton, sister to a marquis and known throughout London? Nothing scared her. Ever. Life was too short to be worrying about what others thought and what might be hiding around the corner. Their father's sudden death many years ago had taught her that.

Chin lifted, she scanned the contents of the letter. Her breath caught in her throat. She grew cognizant of her siblings' gazes upon her.

"No." The word slipped out of her mouth.

"Well, what is your task?" asked Minerva. "Is it truly awful?"

Angel examined the letter again before meeting her sister's worried gaze. She swallowed. "I...I have to get a job."

Made in the USA
Columbia, SC
22 October 2020

23310595R00136